Anonymous

**The Nature, Extent and Province of Human Reason Considered**

Anonymous

**The Nature, Extent and Province of Human Reason Considered**

ISBN/EAN: 9783337368784

Printed in Europe, USA, Canada, Australia, Japan

Cover: Foto ©Andreas Hilbeck / pixelio.de

More available books at **www.hansebooks.com**

THE

NATURE, EXTENT, AND PROVINCE

OF

# HUMAN REASON,

CONSIDERED.

. . . . . . . . . . . . . . . . . . . . . . .

Σκοπει ȣν, μη το Φως το εν Cοι, σκοτος εϛιν.

Ει γαρ το Φως το εν σοι, σκοτος εϛι, το σκοτος ποσον.

. . . . . . . . . . . . . . . . . . . . . .

London:

*SOLD BY*

RICHARD EDWARDS,

NO. 142, BOND-STREET.

1792.

# DEDICATION.

...........................

## TO

## THE RIGHT REVEREND,

## *S A M U E L,*

## LORD BISHOP OF ST. DAVID's.

*MY LORD,*

THE appearance of the following pages, in their prefent form, origi-nates from fome incidental conver-fation, in a fmall circle of friends to *Revealed Religion, Philofophic Truth,* and *Sound Learning ;* a con-

verfation,

verfation, of which your Lordfhip's late CHARGE was the valuable occafion and fource.

To Minds, whofe attachment to the SACRED SCRIPTURES is fomething more than national, or profeffional ; which *feel*, what they admire, and efteem ; the departure of the times, from the obvious principles of divine Revelation, has long been a matter of fincere, and, it is hoped, of benevolent fenfibility ; a fenfibility, which they would be ready, and which indeed they ought, to difavow, were they not perfuaded, that it is founded on the *Venuftum*, the *Honeftum*, the *Decorum* of things. But, in the manly zeal, in the

the liberal firmnefs, in the extenfive erudition, and in the evangelical truths, which they conceive to be difplayed in the above Charge, the almoft defpairing caufe of *genuine*, *apoftolical Chriftianity*, begins to revive.

Very cheerfully do we fubfcribe to the fentiments of a noble author, when he tells us, that, " In what form or manner foever *Criticifm* may appear among us, or *Critics*, chufe to exercife their talents, it can become none, befides the grofsly fuperftitious or ignorant, to be alarmed at this *Spirit*, fo long as it regards the rules of *Decency*. For, from the confideration of antient, as

well

well as modern times, it appears, that the caufe, and intereft, of Critics, is the fame with that of Wit, Learning, and good Senfe."

Under this conviction, we deprecate the *feverity* of the faftidious reader; we folicit the *candour* of thofe, whofe purfuit is *things*, not *founds*. Our appeal is, to the underftanding and the heart. Elegance of compofition, we profefs to admire — Tafte, we approve — but *TRUTH* is our *ultimatum*. Let *That* be fecure, and let Folly, let Sophiftry, let Falfhood be detected and expofed.

But, whatever may be the deference and refpect moft juftly due,

and

and which we are moſt willing to render to the united efforts of a ſet of gentlemen, who have engaged in the arduous and beneficial office of *Reviewers*; whom we may very properly conſider as forming a ſort of *Literary Phalanx*; and whoſe judgments, we could wiſh, for the ſake of Truth and Piety, were as *impartial*, as they are able, we are ſtill of opinion with your Lordſhip, that,

" Religion and Science are very different things; and the objects of different faculties. Science is the object of natural Reaſon; religious Truth, of Faith. Faith, like the natural faculties, may be improved

by

by exercife, but, in its beginning,
it is unqueftionably a diftinct gift of
God*."—

If *Faith*, in the general idea of
it, be confidered, as the unreferved
fubmiffion or furrender of the underftanding and heart to the *revealed
Will of God*--it certainly muft be confidered, as a kind of faculty, entirely
diftinct from what is univerfally
meant by *human Reafon*. Becaufe,
it feems to be the peculiar property,
the province, it *may* be a moral excellency of Faith, in its relation to
the Divine Being, cordially to receive *that*, upon the divine tefti-

* 1 Cor. ii.        Eph. ii. 8.

mony

mony alone, *the reafon* of which it cannot at prefent difcover. It may be one of the higheft exercifes of true goodnefs, to fay, in this cafe, of the fupreme Governor of the world, *Stat pro ratione, voluntas;* the Will of God being the firft ·caufe, and eternal bafis, of all moral obligation.

As to the objection, hereafter fufficiently difcuffed, as if, upon *this* principle, the moral Governor of the univerfe was a mere *arbitrary Being* —we need only remark in this place, that, " A Being, of *infinite* freedom and independency, muft neceffarily act according to his own fovereign will and pleafure. If every thing
received

received its exiftence from him; if every thing, which exifts, be the effect of his Will, and he can do nothing, but *becaufe* he wills it, muft he not be as *arbitrary*, as he is *powerful?* And, though *Will* and *Power*, when confidered as blind or imperfect faculties in man, may pafs for *humour* and *caprice*, yet, as attributes of God, they muft have the *perfection* of God. And, if the Will of God be in the higheft ftate of perfection, *as fuch*, then, we have the higheft reafon to love and adore him, *becaufe* he is *arbitrary*---becaufe he acts according to his own *independent* and *all-perfect Will.*—

Nothing

Nothing can be more evident, my Lord, to thofe who are in the habit of *reflecting*, and *difcriminating* between true and falfe, fpecious and real, than that, as there have been feveral things, which have not had the effence of *Virtue* in them, which have neverthelefs been miftaken for virtue--there are feveral things, which have been miftaken for *Reafon*, which are as far from the thing itfelf, as Scepticifm is from the moft eftablifhed axioms ; or, as the date of the Chinefe empire, from forty thoufand years.

It has been very much the fafhion in all our modern productions, which have the moft diftant reference to

4                           Religion,

Religion, to denominate the prefent age, *The Age of Reafon*; and to panegyrize it, as fuperlatively diftinguifhable for *Liberality of fentiment.* That it may be *The Age of reafoning Pride*, we will not difpute. And, inafmuch as it has been faid, to have the ftrong outline of *Liberality of Sentiment*, we are perfectly agreed with your Lordfhip, that, in this equivocal and undefinable phrafe, " A *profane indifference* is made to pafs for an *accomplifhment.*"

Will your Lordfhip permit us, for the fake of *good humour*, which, we apprehend, is no enemy to true religion, to introduce here a little anecdote, in allufion to your own idea?

idea? The Polifh hiftorians record, that, after the death of *Stephen*, one of the braveft of their kings, there came ambaffadors to *Poland*, from the *Cham of Tartary*, who was a candidate for the Crown. They had inftructions to reprefent to the *Dyet*, " That the *Cham* was a Prince of great power; and that, as to his perfonal qualities, he was temperate and fober. That, being informed there were differences among them about *Religion*, he gave them affurances, that *their Pope fhould be his Pope*, and *their Luther be his Luther*, juft as they pleafed to determine."

b                    To.

To *Liberality of Sentiment*, very clofely in alliance with this, and to uncommon pretenfions to fuperior *Reafon*, we are much indebted for the repeated and various attempts, which have been made upon our civil and ecclefiaftical conftitution. By one of *their* difciples, who announces himfelf the humble echo of a modern Herefiarch and reftlefs Sectary, your Lordfhip was, not long fince, addreffed in the following remarkable ftyle:

"I wifh it could be uttered with a voice, that would penetrate every corner of the nation, and that could roufe *the people* of Britain *to rife* as one man, to *require* that the public
fervice

fervice of Religion be cleanfed from
thefe pollutions," [*meaning the doc-
trinal Articles of our Church*] "which
prefs hard on the confciences of the
moft worthy among the clergy,---
which drive many to infidelity—
which render others indifferent to
Religion---and which keep from the
Church, members, whofe talents,
and whofe weight of character, would
render it eminent fervice."---When-
ever the ftate of the Church fhall
*really need* their affiftance, it will be
very proper, no doubt, to facrifice
*both* for the benefit of *fuch* talents,
and *fuch* characters.—Till then, fo
long as the Public is infulted with
fuch outrageous and inflammatory
effufions as thefe, it will be impoffible

fible for them to forget the comic wit of an *Hudibras*, or the lefs tempered fatire of *The Tale of a Tub*.

We have feen, that, if your Lordfhip ftep forward to affert the fundamental principles of Revelation—*the effential Deity of the Saviour — the Doctrine of Juftification by Faith— and the Neceffity of the Divine Affiftance of the Holy Spirit*, it is afcribed, by a certain defcription of Perfons, to *motives* the moft difingenuous and irreputable. If your Lordfhip enforce upon your Clergy the expediency of an *avowed*, *honeft*, and *fteady* adherence to the national Church, it is to be charged with the odious names of *Bigotry* and *Perfecution*. And, if the effrontery of

its

its opponents be repelled with the contempt it provokes and deferves, the *decent indignation* is to be denominated ecclefiaftical imperioufnefs and infolence.

Leaving, however, fuch writers, and fuch writings, to the expofition of their own illiberality, and to the cenfure, they will be fure to meet with from the moft refpectable and pious divifion of our Diffenting Brethren; your Lordfhip, we prefume, will recollect, it is fomewhere obferved, by the illuftrious and immortal *Bacon*, " Nobis res falubris videtur, et imprimis utilis, fi Tractatus inftituatur fobrius et diligens, qui de ufu Rationis humanæ in Theologicis præcipiat.

piat. Ejufmodi tractatum inter de-
fiderata ponimus; et, *Sophronem*,
five de legitimo ufu Rationis humanæ in divinis nominamus."

Since nothing fo complete, as
what is here infinuated, or propofed,
has yet appeared in the republic of
letters; your Lordfhip may perhaps, on fome future occafion, throw
fuch light on this important fubject,
as may ferve the great caufe of revealed Truth—and fhew, with a
more confummate degree of accuracy
than has hitherto been done, the
exact line of diftinction, where *Rea-*
*fon* may be faid to end, and *Faith* to
begin its operations, in divine fci-
ence. In the mean time, we flat-
ter

ter ourfelves you will condefcend to take this little Treatife into your protection and patronage.

Your Lordfhip is not addreffed, in thefe lines, with the contemptible voice of adulation—of ecclefiaftical bigotry—or of ignorant fuperftition. We addrefs you, as one of the Fathers of our Church—whofe *primary* object is, not its emoluments, nor its dignities, nor its political confequence in the civil conftitution, but the prefervation of its fundamental truths — the perpetuity of its difcipline—and the religious character of its members. As fuch, we venerate your office—we admire your

intellectual

intellectual powers—we refpect your perfon—and we pray for the blef-fing of Heaven upon your indefa-tigable exertions for its honour and fuccefs.

C. D.

D. P.      T. H.

W. J.      J. C.

E. H.      R. E.

# NATURE, EXTENT, AND PROVINCE

OF

# REASON.

## CHAP. I.

*Enquiring, whether there be any thing in the* nature *and* condition *of man, to oblige him to think, that he is not to admit of any doctrines or institutions, as revealed from* God, *but such, as his own Reason can prove to be necessary from the nature of things.*

I BEGIN with enquiring, what there is to *oblige* a man to hold this opinion: because, if there be not some strong and plain proof arising from the *nature* and *condition* of man, to *oblige* him thus to abide by the sole light of his own Reason; it may be so far from being a

B                    duty,

duty, which he owes to God, that it may be reckoned amongft his moft criminal prefumptions. And the pleading for this authority of his own Reafon, may have the guilt of pleading for his greateft vanity. And if *fpiritual pride be the worft fort of pride*, a confident reliance upon our own Reafon, as having a right to determine all matters between God and man, if it fhould prove to be a *groundlefs pretenfion*, bids fair to be reckoned the higheft inftance of the *worft* kind of the worft of fins.

Every other inftance of vanity, every degree of perfonal pride, and felf-efteem, may be a pardonable weaknefs in comparifon of this. For, how fmall is that pride, which only makes us pre-fer our perfonal beauty or merit to that of our fellow-creatures, when compared
with

with a felf-confiding Reafon, which is too haughty to adore any thing in the divine counfels, which it cannot fully comprehend; or to fubmit to any directions from God, but fuch as its own wifdom could prefcribe, or approve? Thus much is certain, that there can be no *Medium* in this matter. The claiming this authority to our own Reafon, muft either be a very great duty, or amongft the greateft of fins.

If it be a *fin*, to admit of any *fecrets* in divine providence—If it be a *crime*, to afcribe wifdom and goodnefs to God in things we cannot comprehend—If it be a *bafenefs* and *meannefs* of fpirit, to believe that God can teach us *better*, or *more* than we can teach ourfelves—If it be a *fhameful apoftacy* from the dignity of our nature, to be humble in the hands

of

of God, to fubmit to any *myfterious pro-vidence* over us, to comply with any other methods of *homage* and *adoration* of him, than fuch as we could of ourfelves contrive and juftify, then it is certainly a great duty to affert and maintain this authority of our own Reafon.

On the other hand; If the profound-eft Humility towards *God*, be the higheft inftance of piety—If every thing within us and without us, if every thing we know of God, every thing we know of ourfelves, preach humility to us, as the foundation of every virtue, as the life and foul of all holinefs—If *fin* had its beginning from *pride*, and *hell* be the effect of it ; if *devils* are what they are through fpiritual pride and felf-conceit, then, we have great reafon to believe, that the claiming this authority to our
Reafon,

Reafon, in oppofition to the revealed wifdom of God, is not a frailty of *flefh* and *blood*, but that fame fpiritual pride, which turned *Angels* into *apoftate* Spirits.

Since therefore this appealing to our own Reafon, as the abfolutely *perfect mea-fure and rule* of all that ought to pafs between God and man, has an *appearance* of a pride of the *worft* kind, and fuch as unites us both in temper and conduct with the fallen fpirits of the kingdom of darknefs, it highly concerns every pleader on that fide, to confider what grounds he proceeds upon ; and to afk himfelf, what there is in the *ftate* and *condition* of human nature, to oblige him to think that nothing can be *divine*, or *holy*, or *neceffary*, in religion, but what *human* Reafon dictates.

I hope the reader will think this a fair
ftate

ftate of the cafe, and that all the light we can have in this matter, muſt arife from a thorough confideration of the *ſtate* and *condition* of man in this world. If, without Revelation, he be free from myſteries as a *moral* and *religious* agent, then he has fome plea from his *ſtate* and *condition* to rejeἀ *revealed* myſteries.

But if, in a ſtate of natural religion, and mere morality, he cannot acknowledge a divine providence, or worſhip and adore God without *as much* implicit faith, and humble fubmiſſion of his Reaſon, as any revealed myſteries require ; then, his *ſtate* and *condition* in the world will condemn his refuſal of any revelation fufficiently atteſted to come from God.

Had mankind continued in a ſtate of *perfeἀ innocence,* without ever failing in

2                                        their

their duty either to God or man, yet even in fuch a ftate, they could never have known what God would, or would not reveal to them, but by fome exprefs revelation from him. And, as God might intend to raife them to fome higher, and unknown ftate of perfection; fo he might raife them to it by the revelation of fuch things as their own Reafon, though innocent and uncorrupt, could not have difcovered.

But if man, in a ftate of *innocence,* could have no pretence to fet himfelf againft divine Revelation; and make his own Reafon the *final judge* of what God could, or could not reveal to him; much lefs has he any pretence for fo doing in his prefent ftate of *fin, ignorance,* and *mifery.* His *nature* and *condition* are fo far from furnifhing him with reafons

againft

againſt Revelation, againſt any *ſupernatu-ral* help from God, that they ſeem to be inconſolable without it ; and every cir-cumſtance of his life prepares him to hope for terms of *mercy* and deliverance from his preſent guilt and miſery, not according to *ſchemes* of his *own* contri-vance, not from his *own knowledge* of the *nature*, and *reaſon*, and *fitneſs* of things, but from ſome *incomprehenſible depth* of divine Goodneſs.

For, if ſin, and miſery, and igno-rance, cannot convince us of our own weakneſs, cannot prepare us to accept of *any methods* of *atoning* for our guilt, but ſuch as our own diſordered Reaſon can ſuggeſt, we are not far from the harden-ed ſtate of thoſe miſerable ſpirits, that make war againſt God.

For, to inſiſt upon the *prerogative* of

our

our own nature, as qualifying us to make our own peace with God, and to reject the *Atonement* which he has provided for us, becaufe we efteem it more fit and reafonable, that our *own Repentance* fhould be fufficient without it, is the fame height of *pride* and *impiety*, as to affirm that we have no need of any repentance at all.

For as mankind, if they had continued in a ftate of *Innocence*, could not have known how their innocence was to be rewarded, or what changes of ftate God intended them for, but as Revelation had difcovered thefe things unto them: fo, after they were *fallen* into a ftate of guilt and fin, they could never know what *effects* it was to have upon them; what *mifery* it would expofe them to; or *when*, or *how*, or *whether* they were

ever

ever to be delivered from it, and made as happy as if they had *never* finned : thefe are things, that nothing but a Revelation from God could teach them.

So that, for a Sinner to pretend to appoint the *atonement* for his own Sins, or to think himfelf able to tell what it *ought* to be, or what *effect* it muft have with God, is as foolifh and vain a prefumption, as if man in *innocence* fhould have pretended to appoint his own method of being changed into a *Cherub*.

The Writers againft Revelation, appeal to the *Reafon* and *Nature* of things, as *infallibly* difcovering every thing that a Revelation from God can teach us.

*If the relations, fay they, between things, and the fitnefs refulting from thence, be not the fole Rule of God's actions, muft not God be an arbitrary Being ? But if God only*
commands

*commands what the nature of things shew to be fit, 'tis scarce possible that men should mistake their duty; since a Mind that is attentive, can as easily distinguish fit from unfit, as the Eye can beauty from deformity.*

It is granted, that there is a fitness and unfitness of actions founded in the nature of things, and resulting from the relations that persons and things bear to one another. It is also granted, that the reasonableness of most of the duties of children to their parents, of parents to their children, and of men to men, is very apparent, from the relation they bear to one another ; and that several of the duties which we owe to God, plainly appear to us, as soon as we acknowledge the relation that is between God and us.

But

But when all this is granted, this *whole argument* proves directly the contrary to that which it is intended to prove.

I readily grant, that the Nature, Reafon, and Relations of things and perfons, and the fitnefs of actions refulting from thence, is the *fole Rule* of God's actions. And I appeal to this one common and confeffed principle, as a fufficient proof that a man cannot thus abide by the *fole Light* of his own Reafon, without contradicting the Nature and Reafon of things, and denying this to be the *fole Rule* of God's actions.

For, if the *fitnefs* of actions be founded in the *nature* of things and perfons, and this fitnefs be the *fole Rule* of God's actions, it is certain that the Rule by which he acts, muft in many inftances be be *entirely inconceivable* by us, fo as not to be known *at all*, and in no inftances *fully* known, or *perfectly* comprehended.

For, if God be to act according to a *fitnefs founded* in the *nature* of things, and nothing can be fit for him to do, but what has its fitnefs founded in his own *divinely perfect* and *incomprebenfible* nature, muft he not neceffarily act by a Rule *above* all human comprehenfion? This argument fuppofes that he cannot do what is *fit* for him to do, unlefs what he does has its *fitnefs* founded in his *own nature;* but if he muft govern his actions by his own nature, he muft act by a *Rule* that is juft as *incomprebenfible* to us *as* his own nature.

And we can be no farther *competent Judges* of the *fitnefs* of the conduct of God, than we are competent judges of

C
the

the divine nature ; and can no more tell what is, or is not *infinitely wife* in God, than we can raife ourfelves to a *flate* of infinite wifdom.

So that, if the *fitnefs* of actions be founded in the *particular nature* of things and perfons, and the fitnefs of God's actions muft arife from that which is *particular* to his nature, then we have, from this argument, the *utmoft certainty* that the *Rule* or *Reafons* of God's actions muft in many cafes be entirely inconceivable by us, and in no cafes perfectly and fully apprehended ; and for this very reafon, becaufe he is not an *arbitrary Being*, that acts by *mere Will*, but is governed in every thing he does, by the reafon and nature of things. For, if he be not arbitrary, but acts according to the nature of things, then

he

he muſt act according to his *own nature*. But if his own Nature muſt be the *Rea-ſon*, *Rule*, and *Meaſure* of his actions; if they be only fit and reaſonable, be-cauſe they are according to this *Rule and Reaſon*, then it neceſſarily follows, that the fitneſs of many of God's actions muſt be incomprehenſible to us, *merely* for this reaſon, becauſe they have their *proper fitneſs;* ſuch a fitneſs as is found-ed in *the divine Nature*.

For, ſuppoſing God to be an arbitra-ry Being, there would then be a bare poſſibility of our comprehending the fitneſs of every thing he required of us. For, as he might act by *mere Will*, ſo he might chuſe to act according to our na-ture, and ſuitable to our comprehen-ſions, and not according to his own na-ture, and infinite perfections.

But,

But, suppofing God not to be an *ar-bitrary Being*, but to act conftantly, as the perfections of his own nature make it *fit* and *reafonable* for him to act, then, there is an utter impoffibility of our comprehending the reafonablenefs and fitnefs of many of his actions.

For inftance ; look at the *reafon* of things, and the *fitnefs* of actions, and tell me how they moved God to create mankind in the ftate and condition they are in. Nothing is more above the Reafon of men, than to explain the rea-fonablenefs and infinite wifdom of God's Providence in creating man of fuch a *form* and *condition*, to go through *fuch* a ftate of things as human life has fhewn itfelf to be. ☞ No revealed myfteries can more exceed the Comprehenfion of man, than the ftate of human life itfelf.

Shew

Shew me according to what *fitnefs*, founded in the *nature* of things, God's infinite wifdom was determined to form you in fuch a manner ; bring you into fuch a world ; and fuffer and preferve *fuch a ftate* of things, as human life is ; and then, you may have fome pretence to believe no revealed doctrines, but fuch as your own Reafon can deduce from the nature of things, and the fit-nefs of actions.

But, whilft our own *form*, whilft *Creation* and *Providence* are depths, which you cannot thus look into, it is ftrangely abfurd to pretend, that God cannot reveal any thing to you as a matter of religion, except your own Reafon can fhew its foundation in the nature and reafon of things.

For

For does not your own *make*, and *con-stitution*, the reasonableness of God's providence, and the *fitness* of the State of human life, as much concern you, as any *revealed* doctrines? Is it not as *unfit* for God to create man in such a *state*, subject to such a *course* of providence, as he cannot *prove* to be founded in the *fitness* and *reasonableness* of things; as to reveal to him such truths, or methods of salvation, as he cannot by any arguments of his own prove to be necessary?

*Revelation*, you say, is on your account, and therefore you ought to see the *reasonableness* and *fitness* of it.—And do not you also say, that God has made you for your *own sake?* ought you not therefore to know the reasonableness and

and fitnefs of God's forming you as you are?—Do not you fay, that providence is for the *fake* of Man? is it not there-fore fit and reafonable, in the nature of things, that there fhould be no *myfteries* or *fecrets* in providence, but that man fhould fo fee its methods, as to be able to prove all its fteps to be conftantly fit and reafonable?

Do not you fay, that the *world* is for the *fake* of man; is it not therefore fit and reafonable that man fhould fee, that the *paft* and *prefent* ftate of the world has been fuch as the reafon and fitnefs of things required it fhould be?

Now, if the *imperfect* ftate of human nature, the *miferies* and *calamities* of this life, the *difeafes* and mortality of human bodies, the *methods* of God's continual providence in governing human affairs,

be

be things that as much concern us, and as nearly relate to us, as any methods of revealed religion; and if thefe be things that we cannot examine or explain, according to any *fitnefs* or *unfitnefs* founded in the *nature* of things, but muft believe a great deal more of the infinite wifdom of God, than we can fo explain; have we any reafon to think, that God cannot, or ought not to raife us out of this unhappy ftate of things; help us to an higher order of life, and exalt us to a nearer enjoyment of himfelf, by any means, but fuch as our own poor Reafon can grope out of the nature and fitnefs of things?

Now *why is it*, that all is thus myfterious and unmeafurable by human Reafon, in thefe matters fo nearly concerning human nature? It is

becaufe

becaufe God is not an *arbitrary Being*, but does that, which the *incomprehenfible Perfections* of his own nature, make it *fit* and *reafonable* for him to do. Do but grant, that nothing can be *fit* for God to do, but what is *according* to his own *infinite perfections;* let but this be the *Rule* of his actions, and then you have the *fulleft* proof, that the fitnefs of his actions muft be *above* our comprehenfion, who can only judge of a *fitnefs* according to our *own perfections;* and then we muft be furrounded with myftery, for this very reafon, becaufe God acts according to a *certain Rule, his own Nature.*

Again : What is the *Nature* of a human Soul; upon what *terms,* and in what manner it is *united* to the body; how far it is *different* from it; how far it is *fubject* to it; what powers and faculties

cultics it *derives* from it, are things,
wherein the *Wifdom* and *Goodnefs* of God,
and the *Happinefs* of man are deeply
concerned. Is it not neceffary that thefe
things fhould have their foundation in
the *reafon* and *fitnefs* of things ? and yet,
who can fhew that this *ftate* of foul and
body *is* founded in the reafon and fitnefs
of things ?

Again : The *Origin* of the foul, at
what time it enters into the body, whether it be *immediately* created at its en-
trance into the body, or comes out of
a *pre-exiftent ftate*, are things that cannot be known from any fitnefs or reafonablenefs founded in the nature of
things ; and yet it is as neceffary to believe this is done according to *certain*
*reafons* of wifdom and goodnefs, as to
believe there is a God.

Now,

Now, who can fay that it is the fame thing, whether human fouls are created *immediately* for human bodies, or whe‑ ther they come into them out of fome *pre-exiftent ftate?* For aught we know, • one of thefe ways may be exceeding *fit* and *wife*, and the other as entirely *unjuft* and *unreafonable*; and yet, when Reafon examines either of thefe ways, it finds itfelf *equally perplexed* with dif‑ ficulties, and knows not which to chufe: but if fouls be immaterial [as all philo‑ fophy now proves] it muft be one of them.

And perhaps, the reafon why God has revealed fo little of thefe matters in holy Scripture itfelf, is, becaufe any more particular revelation of them, would but have perplexed us with great‑ er difficulties, as not having capacities or

ideas

ideas to *comprehend* fuch things. For, as all our natural knowledge is confined to ideas borrowed from *experience*, and the ufe of our *fenfes* about *human things ;* as Revelation can only teach us things that have fome likenefs to what we already know; as our notions of equity and juftice are very limited, and confined to certain actions between man and man; fo, if God had revealed to us more particularly, the *origin* of our fouls, and the *reafon* of their ftate in human bodies, we might perhaps have been expofed to greater difficulties by fuch knowledge, and been lefs able to vindicate the juftice and goodnefs of God, than we are by our prefent ignorance.

Again ; the origin of *Sin* and *Evil*, or how it entered into the world confiftently fistently with the infinite wifdom of God, is a myftery of *natural religion*, which Reafon cannot unfold. For, who can fhew from the *reafon* and *nature* of things, that it was *fit* and *reafonable*, for the Providence of God to fuffer fin and evil to enter, and continue in the world as they have ? Here therefore, the Man of natural religion muft drop his method of reafoning from the nature and fitnefs of things; and that, in an article of the higheft concern to the moral world; and be as mere a believer, as he that believes the moft incomprehenfible myftery of revealed religion.

Now, as there have been in the feveral ages of the world, fome *impatient*, *reftlefs*, and *prefuming* fpirits, who, becaufe they could not, in thefe points, explain the juftice of God's providence,

D                    have

have taken refuge in horrid *Atheism :* So, they made juft the fame *fober ufe* of their Reafon, as our *modern unbelievers,* who, becaufe they cannot comprehend as they would, the *fitnefs* and *neceffity* of certain chriftian doctrines, refign themfelves up to a hardened *Infidelity.* For, ☞ It is juft as wife and reafonable to allow of no myfteries in *Revelation,* as to allow of no myfteries or fecrets in *Creation* and *Providence.*

—To proceed : If the *fitnefs of actions be founded in the nature and relations of Beings,* then nothing can be fit for God to do, but fo far as it is fit for the *Governor of all created beings,* whether on earth, or in any other part of the univerfe ; and he cannot act fitly towards mankind, but by acting as is fit for the Governor of all beings.

Now,

Now, what is fit for the *Governor* of *all created nature* to do, in this or that particular part of his creation, is as much above our Reaſon to *tell*, as it is above our power to *govern* all beings. And how *Mankind* ought to be governed, with relation to the whole creation, of which they are ſo ſmall a part, is a matter equally above our knowledge; becauſe we know not how they are a part of the whole, or what relation they bear to any other part, or how their ſtate affects the whole, or any other part, any more than we know what Beings the whole conſiſts of.

Now, there is nothing that we know with more certainty, than that God is Governor of the whole, and that Mankind are a part of the whole; and that the uniformity and harmony of divine

Providence,

Providence, muft arife from his infinitely
wife government of the whole; and therefore we have the utmoft certainty, that we
are *vaftly incompetent* judges of the fitnefs
or unfitnefs of any methods, which God
ufes in the government of fo fmall a
part of the univerfe as mankind are.

For, if the actions of God cannot
have their *proper fitnefs,* unlefs they are
according to the *incomprehenfible greatnefs*
of his *own Nature,* and according to his
incomprehenfible greatnefs, as *Lord* and
*Governor* of all created nature; have we
not the moft undeniable certainty, that
the fitnefs of the divine Providence over
mankind, muft be a fecret only to be
adored, but never comprehended, in this
life?—

Again, if the *fitnefs of actions be founded
in the Relations of beings to one another,*
then

then the fitnefs of the actions of God's providence over mankind, muft be in many inftances *altogether myfterious and incomprehenfible to us.*

For the *relation* which God bears to mankind, as their *all-perfect Creator* and continual *Preferver,* is a relation that we conceive as imperfectly, and know as little of, as we do of any of the divine attributes. When we compare it to that of a *Father* and his children, a *Prince* and his fubjects, a *Proprietor* and his property, we have explained it in the beft manner we can ; but ftill have left it as much a *fecret,* as we do the divine nature, when we fay it is *infinitely* fuperior to every thing that is *finite.*

We know with certainty, feveral *effects* of this relation ; as, that it puts us under the care and protection of a wife, and

juft,

juft, and merciful Providence, and demands from us the higheft inftances of
humility, duty, adoration and thankf-
giving. But, what it is in its own nature, what kind of *ftate*, or degree of
*dependency* it fignifies; what it is, to
exift in and by God; what it is, to fee
by a *light* that is his, to act by a *power*
from him, to live by a *life* in him; is,
what we conceive as *imperfectly*, as what
it is to be in the *third heavens*, or to hear
words that cannot be uttered.

But, if this relation confift in thefe
*inconceivable* things, in a communica-
tion of *life*, *light*, and *power*; if thefe
be enjoyed in God, and in ourfelves;
our own, and yet his, in a manner not
to be explained by any thing that we
ever heard, or faw; then, we muft neceffarily be poor judges of what is fit
for

for God to require of us, becaufe of this *relation.* It teaches us nothing, but the fuperficialnefs of our own knowledge, and the unfathomable depths of the divine perfections.

It is becaufe of this incomprehenfible Relation between God and his creatures, that we are unavoidably ignorant of what God may juftly require of us, either in a ftate of *Innocence* or *Sin.* For, as the fitnefs of actions between Beings *related,* muft refult from their refpective Natures, fo the incomprehenfibility of the Divine Nature, on which the Relation between God and man is founded, makes it utterly impoffible for us to fay, what *kind* of *homage,* or *worſhip,* he may *fitly* require of man in a ftate of *innocence;* or what *different* worſhip and homage

mage he may, or muſt require of men
as *ſinners*.

As to the obligations of moral or fo-
cial duties, which have their foundation
in the conveniences of this life, and the
ſeveral relations we bear to one another,
theſe are the ſame in the ſtate of *Innocence* or *Sin;* and we know, that we truly
act according to the Divine Will, when
we act according to what theſe relations
require of us.

But the queſtion is, What diſtinct
kind of *Homage*, or *Service*, or *Worſhip*,
God may require us to render to Him,
either in a ſtate of *Innocence* or *Sin*, on
account of that Relation he bears to
us as an all-perfect Creator and Governor ?

But this is a queſtion, that God alone
can reſolve.

Human

Human Reafon cannot enter into it; it has no principle to proceed upon in it. For as the *neceffity* of Divine Worfhip and Homage, fo the *particular matter* and *manner* of it, muft have its reafon in the Divine Nature.

*Sacrifice*, if confidered only as an *human Invention*, could not be proved to be a reafonable fervice. Yet, confidered as a *Divine Inftitution*, it would be the greateft folly not to receive it as a reafonable fervice. For, as we could fee no reafon for it, if it were of human invention, fo we fhould have the greateft reafon to comply with it, becaufe it was of Divine Appointment. Not as if the Divine Appointment altered the *nature* and *fitnefs* of things; but, becaufe nothing has the *nature* and *fitnefs* of Divine Worfhip, but *becaufe* it is of Divine Appointment.

Man

Man, therefore, had he continued in a ftate of Innocence, and without Revelation, might have lived in an awful fear, and pious regard of God, and obferved every duty both of moral and civil life, as an act of obedience to him. But he could have no foundation either to invent any particular *matter* or *manner* of Divine Worfhip himfelf, or to reject any that was appointed by God as *unneceffary.* It would have been ridiculous to have pleaded his innocence, as having no need of a Divine Worfhip. For who can have greater reafon, or be fitter to worfhip God, than innocent Beings? It would have been more abfurd to have objected the fufficiency and perfection of their Reafon; for why fhould men reject a *revealed method and manner* of Divine Worfhip and Service, becaufe God had

had given them Senfe and Reafon of their own fufficient for the duties of fo-cial and civil life?

And as Reafon, in a ftate of fuch in-nocence and perfection, could not have any pretence to ftate, or appoint, the matter or manner of Divine Worfhip, fo when the ftate of innocence was changed for that of fin, it then became more difficult for bare Reafon to know what kind of homage, or worfhip, could be acceptable to God from Sin-ners.

For, what the *Relation* betwixt God and Sinners makes it fit and reafonable for God to require or accept of them, can-not be determined by human Reafon.

This is a *new State*, and the founda-tion of a *new Relation ;* and nothing can be fit *for God to do in it, but what has its*

*fitnefs*

*fitnefs refulting from it.* We have nothing to help our conceptions of the
forementioned *relative charaƐers* of God,
as our *Governor* and *Prcferver,* but what
we derive from our idea of human
*Fathers* and *Governors.* Which idea
only helps us to comprehend thefe *relations,* juft as our idea of human power
helps us to comprehend the *Omnipotence*
of God. For a father, or governor, no
more reprefents the *true ftate* of God as
our *Governor* and *Preferver,* than our
living in our Father's *family,* reprefents
the *true manner* of our living in God.

Thefe Relations are both very plain,
and very myfterious; they are very plain
and certain, as to the *reality* of their
exiftence; and highly myfterious and
inconceivable, as to the *manner* of their
exiftence.

That

That which is *plain* and *certain*, in thefe relative characters of God, clearly shews our obligations to every inftance of *duty, homage, adoration, love* and *gratitude.*

* And that, which is *myfterious* and *inconceivable* in them, is a juft and folid foundation of that *profound humility, awful reverence, internal piety,* and *tremendous fenfe* of the divine Majefty, with which devout and pious perfons think of God, and affift at the *offices* and *inftitutions* of Religion. Which excites in them a higher zeal for doctrines and inftitutions of divine Revelation, than for all things human ; which fills them with regard and reverence for all *things, places,* and *offices,* that are either by divine or human authority appointed, to affift

E                                     and

and help their defired intercourfe with God.

And, if fome people, by a *long* and *ftrict* attention to *Reafon, clear ideas*, the *fitnefs* and *unfitnefs* of things, have at laft arrived at a demonftrative certainty, that all thefe fentiments of piety and devotion are mere *bigotry, fuperftition*, and *enthufiafm*; I fhall only now obferve, that *youthful extravagance, paffion*, and *debauchery*, by their own *natural tendency*, without the affiftance of any other guide, feldom fail of making the fame difcovery. And, though it is not reckoned any reflection upon *great Wits*, when they hit upon the fame thought, yet it may feem fome difparagement of that *Reafon* and *Philofophy*, which teaches *old men* to think and judge the fame of Religion,

gion, as *paſſion* and *extravagance* teach the young.——

To return: As there is no ſtate in human life, that can give us a true idea of any of the forementioned relative characters of God, ſo this relative ſtate of God towards ſinners is ſtill more remote, and leſs capable of being truly comprehended by any thing obſervable in the relations betwixt a *judge* and criminals, *a creditor* and his debtors, a *phyſician* and his patients, a *father* or *prince*, and their diſobedient children and ſubjects.

For none of theſe ſtates ſeparately, nor all of them jointly conſidered, give us any juſt idea, either of the *nature* and *guilt* of ſin, or how God is to deal with ſinners, on the account of the relation he bears to them.

And

And to afk, whether God, in punifhing finners, acts as a *phyfician* towards
patients, or as a *creditor* towards debtors,
or as a *prince* towards rebels, or a *judge*
over criminals, is the fame weaknefs, as
to afk, whether God, as our *continual*
*preferver*, acts as our parents, from whom
we have our *maintenance*, or as a prince,
who only *protects* us. For, as the *mainte-*
*nance* and *protection*, that we receive from
our parents and prince, are not proper
and true reprefentations of the *nature*
and *manner* of our *prefervation* in God,
but only the propereft words that human
language affords us, to fpeak of things
not human, but divine and inconceivable in their own proper natures: fo a
*phyfician* and his patients, a *creditor* and
his debtors, a *prince* and his rebels, or a
*judge* over criminals, neither feparately
nor

nor jointly confidered, are proper and
ftrict reprefentations of the *reafons* and
*manner* of God's proceedings with finners, but only help us to a more proper
language to fpeak about them, than any
other ftates of human life.

To afk, whether *Sin* hath folely the
*nature* of an *offence*, againft a prince or
a father, and fo is pardonable by
mere goodnefs ; whether it be like an
*error* in a *road* or *path*, and fo is entirely
at an end, when the right path is
taken ; whether its guilt hath the nature of a debt, and fo is capable of
being difcharged, juft as a debt is ;
whether it affects the foul, as a *wound*
or *difeafe* affects the body, and fo ought
only to move God to act as a good
phyfician ? all thefe queftions are as vain
as

as to afk, Whether knowledge in God be
really *thinking*, or his nature a real *fubftance*. For as his knowledge and nature
cannot be *ftrictly* defined, but are capable of being fignified by the terms,
*thinking* and *fubftance*, fo the nature of
fin is not *ftrictly reprefented* under any of
thefe characters, but is capable of receiving *fome reprefentation* from every one
of them.

When Sin is faid to be an *offence* againft
God, it is to teach us, that we have infinitely more reafon to dread it on *God's
account*, than to dread any offence againft
our parents, or governors.

When it is compared to a *debt*, it is to
fignify, that our fins make us accountable to God, not in the *fame manner*, but
with the fame certainty, as a debtor is
anfwer-

anfwerable to his creditor; and becaufe it has fome likenefs to a debt, which of ourfelves we are not able to pay.

When it is compared to a *wound*, or difeafe in the body, it is not to teach us, that it may as eafily be healed as bodily wounds, but, to help us to conceive the greatnefs of its evil; that, as difeafes bring death to the body, fo fin brings a worfe kind of death upon the foul.

Since therefore, the *nature* and *guilt* of fin can only fo far be known, as to make it highly to be *dreaded*, but not fo known as to be *fully* underftood, by any thing we can compare it to—

Since the *relation* which God bears to *finners*, can only be fo known, as to make it highly reafonable to proftrate ourfelves before him, in every inftance of
humility

humility and penitence; but not so fully known, as to teach us how, or in what manner, God muſt deal with us; it plainly follows, that, if God be not an *arbitrary* Being, but acts according to a *fitneſs*, *reſulting* from this relation, then he muſt, in this reſpect, act by a *Rule* or *Reaſon* known only to himſelf, and ſuch as we cannot *poſſibly* ſtate from the *reaſon* and *nature* of things.

This account is ſufficient to ſhew us, with how little reaſon and regard to the nature of things, *unbelievers* object againſt the *Atonement* for ſins by Jeſus Chriſt.

Their firſt objection is, that *Repentance alone* is a *ſufficient atonement* for ſin. Were they to affirm, that *ſinning Angels* might ſufficiently regain their former perfection by a *bare wiſh*, they would

proceed

proceed as much according to their knowledge of the nature of things, as in affirming, that *finful man* can *merit* the pardon of his fins by his *own repentance*. I fay, *merit*, becaufe they, who hold re-pentance to be a *fufficient title* to pardon, can be no farther certain of it, than fo far as they are *certain*, that it *merits* it. And, according to this *fcheme*, the *peni-tent*, who thinks he has repented, need not *beg* of God to have compaffion upon him, but *demands* a due, which the *na-ture of things* gives him a right to claim.

But if the nature of things, and the fitnefs of actions refulting from their relations, is to be the rule of our Reafon, then *Reafon* muft be here at a full ftop, and can have no more light or know-ledge to proceed upon, in ftating the *na-*

*ture,*

*ture*, the *guilt*, or proper *atonement* of fin in men, than of fin in *Angels*.

For *Reafon*, by confulting the *nature* and *fitnefs* of things, can no more tell us, what the *guilt* of fin is; what *hurt* it does us; how far it *enters* into, and *alters* our very nature; what *contrariety to*, and *feparation* from God, it neceffarily brings upon us; or what *fupernatural* means are, or are not, neceffary to abolifh it; our *Reafon* can no more tell this, than our *fenfes* can tell us, what is the *inward*, and what is the *outward* light of Angels.

Afk Reafon, what *effect* fin has upon the foul? and it can tell you no more, than if you had afked, what effect the *omniprefence* of God has upon the foul?

Afk

Afk Reafon, and the nature of things, what is, or ought to be, the *true nature* of an atonement for fin; how far it is like *paying* a *debt*, *reconciling* a *difference*, or *healing* a *wound*, or how far it is diffe-‘rent from them ? and it can tell you no more, than if you had afked, what is the *true degree* of power that *preferves* us in exiftence ; how far it is *like* that which at firft created us, and how far it is *diffe-rent* from it ?

All thefe enquiries are, by the nature of things, made impoffible to us; and we can only become *knowing* and *philo-fophers*, in thefe matters, by deferting our Reafon, and giving ourfelves up to *vifion* and *imagination*.

And we have as much authority from the reafon and nature of things, to ap-peal to *hunger* and *thirft*, and *fenfual plea-*

5                                    *fure,*

*fure,* to tell us *how* our fouls fhall live in the beatifick prefence of God, as to appeal to our *Reafon* and *Logick,* to demonftrate how fin is to be *atoned,* or the foul *altered, prepared,* and *purified,* for future happinefs.

For God has no more given us our Reafon, to *fettle* the nature of an atonement for fin; or to find out what can, or cannot, take away its guilt, than he has given us *fenfes* and *appetites* to ftate the nature, or difcover the ingredients, of future happinefs.

And he, who rejects the *atonement* for fins made by the Son of God, as *needlefs,* becaufe he cannot prove it to be *neceffary,* is as extravagant, as he that fhould deny that God created him by his *only Son,* becaufe he did not *remember* it. For our Memory is as proper a faculty

culty to tell us, whether God at firft created us, and all things, by his only Son, as our *Reafon* is to tell us, whether we ought to be reftored to God, with, or without the mediation of Jefus Chrift.

This objection, therefore, againft any *fupernatural* means of atoning for fin, taken from the *fufficiency* of our own Repentance, is as *clear* and *philofophical,* as that *knowledge* which is without *any ideas ;* and as juftly to be relied upon, as that *conclufion* which has no *premifes.—*

But, there are two more objections urged againft the atonement for fin, made by Jefus Chrift. *Firft,* as it is an *human facrifice, which nature itfelf abhors ;* and which was looked upon as the great abomination of idolatrous *pagan* worfhip.

F                    The

The *cruelty, injuftice,* and *impiety,* of fhedding *human* blood in the facrifices of the *pagan* religion, is fully granted: but *Reafon* cannot thence bring the fmalleft objection againft the facrifice of Chrift, as it was *human.*

For how can Reafon be more difregarded, than in fuch an argument as this? The *Pagans* were unjuft, cruel, and impious, in offering human blood to their falfe gods, therefore the true God cannot receive any *human* facrifice for fin, or allow any perfons to die, as a punifhment for fin.

For, if no human facrifice can be fit for God to receive, becaufe human facrifices, as parts of *pagan* worfhip, were unjuft and impious; then it would follow, that the *mortality,* to which all mankind are appointed by God, muft have

have the *fame cruelty* and *injuftice* in it.
Now, that *death* is a punifhment for fin,
and that all mankind are by death offer-
ed as a *facrifice* for fin, is not only a doctrine of revealed Religion, but the plain
dictate of Reafon. For, though it is
Revelation alone that can teach us, how
God threatened death as the punifhment
of a particular fin, yet Reafon muft be
obliged to acknowledge, that men die,
becaufe they are finners. But if men
die, becaufe they are finners, and Reafon itfelf muft receive this, as the moft
juftifiable caufe of Death; then Reafon
muft allow, that the death of all mankind is appointed by the true God, as
a *facrifice* for fin. But, if Reafon muft
acknowledge the death of all mankind
as a facrifice for fin, then it can have no
juft

juſt objection againſt the ſacrifice of Chriſt, *becauſe* it was *human.*

Revelation, therefore, teaches nothing more hard to be believed on this point, than Reaſon teaches. For, if it be juſt and fit in God, to *appoint* and *devote* all men to death, as the proper *puniſhment* of their ſins; how can it be proved to be unjuſt and unfit in God, to receive the death of Jeſus Chriſt, for the ſame ends ?

. I do not pretend to prove the *fitneſs* and *reaſonableneſs* of God's procedure in the *mortality* of mankind; Revelation is not under any neceſſity of proving this; becauſe it is no difficulty that ariſes from Revelation, but equally belongs to natural religion; and both of them muſt acknowledge it to be fit and reaſonable;

not

not becaufe it can be proved to be fo from the nature of things, but is to be believed to be fo, by faith and piety.

But, if the neceffary faith and piety of natural religion, will not fuffer us to think it *inconfiftent* with the juftice and goodnefs of God, to appoint all man-kind victims to death on the account of fin, then *Reafon*, or *natural Religion*, can have no objection againft the facrifice of Chrift, as it is an *human facrifice*.

And all that *Revelation* adds to *natural religion*, on the point of *human* facrifices, is only this; the knowledge of *one*, that gives *merit*, *effect*, and *fanctification*, to all the reft.

*Secondly*, It is objected, that the Atone-ment made by Jefus Chrift, reprefents God as punifhing the *innocent*, and acquitting

quitting the *guilty*; or, as punifhing the innocent *inflead* of the guilty.

But this proceeds all upon miftake: for the atonement made by Jefus Chrift, though it procures pardon for the guilty, yet it does not acquit them, or excufe them from any punifhment, or fuffering for fin, which *Reafon* could impofe upon them. Natural religion calls men to repentance for their fins: the atonement made by Jefus Chrift, does not acquit them from it, or pardon them without it; but calls them to a *feverer* repentance, a *higher* felf-punifhment and penance, than natural religion, alone, prefcribes. So that *Reafon* cannot accufe this atonement, of *acquitting* the guilty; fince it brings them under a neceffity of doing *more*, and performing a

*feverer*

*feverer* repentance than Reafon, alone, can impofe upon them.

. God therefore does not, by this proceeding, as is unreafonably faid, . fhew his *diflike* of the *innocent*, and his *approbation* of the *wicked*.

For how can God be thought to punifh our bleffed Saviour out of *diflike*, if his fufferings be reprefented of fuch infinite merit with him? Or, how can he fhew thereby his *approbation* of the guilty, whofe repentance is not *acceptable* to him, till recommended by the infinite merits of Jefus Chrift?

*Reafon* therefore has nothing that it can juftly object againft the atonement made by our bleffed Lord, either as it was an *human facrifice*, or as *freeing* the *guilty*, and punifhing the innocent in their ftead ; becaufe this very Sacrifice

calls

calls people to a *higher state* of suffering and punishment for sin, than *Reason*, alone, could oblige them to undergo.

- As to the fitness and reasonableness of our blessed Lord's sufferings, as he was God and man; and the *nature* and *degree* of their worth; Reason can no more enter into this matter, or *disprove* any thing about it, than it can enter into the state of the whole creation, and shew, how it could, or could not, be in the whole, better than it is.

For you may as well ask any of your *senses*, as ask your *Reason* this principal question, *Whether any supernatural mean be necessary for the atonement of the sins of mankind?* Or, supposing it necessary, whether the *mediation, death,* and *inter-*

cession

*ceſſion* of Jeſus Chriſt, as God and man, be that true ſupernatural mean?

For, as the fitneſs or unfitneſs of any *ſupernatural* means, for the atonement of ſin, muſt reſult from the *incompreben-ſible relation* God bears to ſinners ; as it muſt have ſuch *neceſſity, worth,* and *dignity,* as this relation *requires,* and becauſe it requires it; it neceſſarily follows, that, if God act according to *this relation,* the *fitneſs* of his actions cannot be according to *our comprehenſion.*—

Again: Suppoſing ſome *ſupernatural means* to be neceſſary, for deſtroying the guilt and power of ſin; or that the *mediation, ſufferings,* and *interceſſion,* of the Son of God incarnate, be the true ſupernatural means, it neceſſarily follows, that a Revelation of ſuch, or any other *ſupernatural* means, cannot poſ-
fibly

fibly be made obvious to our Reafon and Senfes, as the things of human life, or the tranfactions amongft men are; but can only be fo revealed, as to become juft occafions of our *faith, humility, adoration,* and *pious refignation,* to the divine wifdom and goodnefs.

For, to fay that fuch a thing is *fupernatural,* is only faying, that it is fomething, which, by the *neceffary ftate* of our own nature, we are as incapable of knowing, as we are incapable of feeing *fpirits.*

If therefore fupernatural and divine things be ever revealed to us, their *nature* cannot poffibly be revealed to us; that is, they cannot be revealed to us, as they are in their *own nature:* for if they could, fuch things would not be

*fuperna—*

*supernatural,* but such as were suited to our capacities.

If an *Angel* could appear to us, as it is in its own nature, then we should be *naturally* capable of seeing angels ; but, because our nature is not *capable* of such a sight, and angels are, as to us, *supernatural* objects; therefore, when *angels* appear to men, they must appear in some *human,* or *corporeal* form, that their appearance may be suited to our capacities.

. It is just thus, when any *supernatural* or *divine* matter is revealed by God : it can no more possibly be revealed to us, as it is in its *own nature,* than an *Angel* can appear to us, or make itself visible by us, as it is in its own nature ; but such supernatural matter can only be revealed to us, by being represented to

us

us by fomething that we already *natu-rally* know.

Thus, Revelation teaches us this *fu-pernatural* matter; that Jefus Chrift is making *perpetual interceffion for us in hea-ven.* For Chrift's *real ftate,* or *manner* of exiftence with God in heaven, in regard to his Church, cannot, as it is in its *own nature,* be defcribed to us; it is in this refpect *ineffable,* and *incomprehenfible.* And therefore, this high and incon-ceivable manner of Chrift's exiftence with God in heaven, in regard to his church, is revealed to us under an idea, which gives us the trueft reprefentation of it, that we are capable of; *viz.* the idea of a *perpetual interceffion* for his church.

But, if any one fhould thence infer, that the Son of God muft therefore
either

either be always upon his knees in acts of *mental* or *vocal* prayer, or *proſtrate* in ſome humble form of a ſupplicant, he would make a very weak inference.

' Becauſe this revealed idea of Chriſt, as a perpetual Interceſſor in heaven, is only a comparative repreſentation of ſomething, that cannot be *directly* and *plainly* known, as it is in its own nature ; and only teaches us, how to believe ſomething, though imperfectly, yet *truly* and *uſefully* of an *incomprehenſible* matter.

Juſt as our own ideas of *wiſdom* and *goodneſs* do not teach us what the divine wiſdom and goodneſs are in their *own natures ;* but only help us to believe ſomething *truly* and *uſefully* of thoſe perfecti

G                         ons

ons of God, which are in themfelves inconceivable by us.

But then, there is no inferring any
thing from thefe ideas, by which divine
and fupernatural things are reprefented
to us, only the *truth* and *certainty* of
that *likenefs* under which they are reprefented.

Thus, from our own idea of goodnefs
in ourfelves, we can infer nothing concerning goodnefs, as it is a perfection
inherent in God, but only this, that
there certainly is in God fome *inconceivable, infinite* perfection, *truly anfwerable*
to that which we call goodnefs in our-
feves, though as *infinitely* different from
it, as *Omnipotence* is infinitely different
from all that we *naturally* know of
*power.*

But

But then, we can proceed no farther than to the *truth* and *certainty* of this *likeness* ; we cannot by any farther considerations of the *nature* and *manner* of goodnefs, as it is in ourfelves, infer any thing farther, as to the *nature* and *manner* of the *divine goodnefs*. This is as impoffible, as to ftate the real nature and manner of *Omnipotence*, by confidering the *particulars* of *human power*.

In like manner, our revealed idea of Jefus Chrift as an *Interceffor* for us in heaven, gives us the utmoft certainty that he is in heaven for our benefit, in a manner *truly* and *fully* anfwerable to that of a *powerful Interceffor*. But if, from confidering our own ideas of *human Interceffors*, we fhould thence pretend to infer the *real fupernatural* manner of Chrift's exiftence in heaven, we fhould

fall

fall into the fame abfurdity, as if we un-
dertook to reprefent the *true* nature of
*Omnipotence*, by confidering what we
knew of the *nature* and *manner* of human
power.

Again: When it is revealed to us,
that the bleffed Jefus is the one *Mediator* between God and man; that, he is
the *Atonement*, the *Propitiation*, and *Satisfaction* for our fins: thefe expreffions
only teach us *as much* about fo great a
myftery, as *human* language can reprefent. But, they do not teach us the
*real* or *perfect* nature of Chrift's *ftate* between God and finners. For that,
being a *divine* and *fupernatural* matter,
cannot be revealed to us as it is in its
own *Nature*, any more than the *effence* of
God can be made *vifible* to our eyes.

But

But thefe expreffions teach us thus much with certainty, that there is in the *ftate* of Chrift between God and finners, fomething infinitely and inconceivably beneficial to us; and *truly anfwerable* to all that we mean by *mediation, atonement, propitiation,* and *fatisfaction.*

And though the *real, internal manner,* of this mediation and atonement, as it is in its *own nature,* is *incomprehenfible* by us, yet this does not leffen our knowledge of the *truth* and *certainty* of it; any more than the *incomprehenfibility* of the divine nature leffens our *certainty* of its real exiftence.

And as our idea of God, though confifting of incomprehenfible perfections, helps us to a real and certain knowledge of the divine nature; and, though all myfterious, is yet the folid foundation of of all piety; fo our idea of Jefus Chrift, as our *mediator* and *atonement*, though it be incomprehenfible in itfelf, as to its real nature, yet helps us to a *certain* and *real* knowledge of Chrift, as our *mediator* and *atonement;* and, though full of myftery, is yet full of motives to the higheft degrees of piety, devotion, love, and gratitude unto God.

All objections therefore, raifed from difficulties about the nature of *atonements, propitiations,* and *fatisfactions,* as thefe words are ufed to fignify in human life, and common language, are vain, and entirely groundlefs.

For all thefe objections proceed upon this fuppofition, that *atonement,* or *fatisfaction,* when attributed to Jefus Chrift, fignify neither *more* nor *lefs,* than when they are ufed as terms in *human laws,* or

in

in *civil* life.—Take away this supposition, and all objections are entirely re-
moved with it.

Thus, it is thought an unanswerable
difficulty in the present case, How *sins
freely pardoned, could want any expiation ?*
Or how, after a full *equivalent paid, and
adequate satisfaction given, all could be
mercy and pure forgiveness ?*

And yet all this difficulty is founded
upon this absurd supposition, that atonement and satisfaction, when attributed
to Jesus Christ, signify neither more nor
less, than atonements and satisfactions,
when spoken of in human laws, and human life.

. Which is full as absurd, as to suppose,
that *power* and *life*, when attributed to
God, signify neither more nor less, than
when they are spoken of men: for there

is

is no reaſon why we ſhould think there is any thing myſterious and incompre-henſible in *power* and *life*, when attri-buted to God; but what is the ſame reaſon for our thinking, that *atonement* and *ſatisfaction*, when aſcribed to the Son of God, muſt be myſterious and incomprehenſible.

To return : I have granted this great principle, *That the relations of things and perſons, and the fitneſs reſulting from thence, are the ſole Rule of God's actions:* and I have granted it upon this ſuppoſition, that it muſt thence follow, that God muſt act according to his *own Nature;* and therefore nothing could be fit for God to do, or worthy of him, but what had the reaſon of its fitneſs in his own nature: and if ſo, then the *Rule* of his actions could not fall within *our Com-*

4 *prehenſion.*

*prehenfion.* And confequently, *Reafon alone,* could not be a *competent judge* of God's proceedings; or fay, what God might, or might not, require of us.

But though I have thus far, and for this reafon, granted the *Nature* and *Relations* of things and beings, to be *the Rule* of God's actions, becaufe that plainly fuppofes, that therefore his *own Nature* muft be the rule of his actions; yet fince our modern oppofers of revealed doctrines of religion, hold it in another fenfe, and mean by it, I know not what *eternal, immutable* reafons and relations of things, *independent* of any Being, and which are a *common rule and law of God and man,* I entirely declare againft this, as an erroneous and groundlefs opinion.

Thus,

Thus, when an objector fays, *If the relations between things, and the fitnefs refulting from thence, be not the fole rule of God's actions, muft be not be an arbitrary being?* as he here means fome *eternal, immutable relations, independent* of God; fo, to fuppofe, that God cannot be a *wife* and *good* being, unlefs fuch eternal, independent relations, be the *fole rule* of his actions, is as erroneous, as to affirm, that God cannot be *omnifcient*, unlefs *mathematical demonftrations* be his *fole manner* of knowing all things. And it is juft as reafonable to fix God's knowledge *folely* in mathematical demonftrations, that we may thence be affured of his *infallible knowledge,* as to make I know not what independent relations of things, the *fole rule* of his actions, that we may

thence

thence be affured, he is not an *arbitrary*, out a wife and good Being.

And we have as ftrong reafons to be-lieve God to be, in the higheft degree, • *wife* and *good*, without knowing on *what* his wifdom and goodnefs are founded ; as we have to believe him to be *omni-fcient*, and *eternal*, without knowing on *what* his *omnifcience* is founded ; or to *what* his *eternity* is owing. And we have the fame reafon to hold it a vain and fruitlefs enquiry, to afk, what *obliges* God to be *Wife* and *Good*, as to afk what obliges him to be *Omnifcient*, or *Eternal*.

And, as it would be abfurd to afcribe the *Exiftence* of God to *any Caufe*, or found it upon any *independent Relations* of things, fo it is the fame abfurdity, to afcribe the infinite wifdom and goodnefs

nefs of God to *any caufe*, or found them upon any independent relations of things.

Nor do we any more *lofe* the notion, or *leffen* the certainty of the Divine Wif- dom and Goodnefs, becaufe we cannot fay on *what* they are founded, or to *what* they are to be afcribed, than we *lofe* the notion of God, or render his exiftence *uncertain*, becaufe it cannot be founded on any thing, or afcribed to any caufe.

And as, in our account of the exift- ence of things, we are obliged to have recourfe to a Being, whofe exiftence muft not be afcribed to *any Caufe*, becaufe every thing cannot have a caufe, no more than every thing can be created; fo, in our account of *Wifdom* and *Good- nefs*, there is the fame neceffity of hav- ing recourfe to an infinite Wifdom and Goodnefs, that never *began* to be, and that

that is as different as to its *reason* and *manner* of exiftence, from all other wif-dom and goodnefs, which have a begin-ning, as the *exiftence* of God is *different* from the exiftence of the creatures.

But, if it be neceffary to hold, that there is an infinite wifdom and goodnefs that *never began* to be, then it is as ne-ceffary to affirm, that fuch wifdom and goodnefs can no more be *founded* upon the *relations* of things, than the *unbe-ginning exiftence* of God can be *founded* upon the exiftence of things. And to feek for any *reafons* of a wifdom and goodnefs, that could not begin to be, but were always in the *fame infinite* ftate, is like feeking the caufe of that, which can have no caufe, or afking, *what* it is that *contains* infinity.

II But,

But, to derive the wifdom and goodnefs of God from the directions he receives from the *Relations* of things, becaufe our wifdom and goodnefs are directed by them, is as weak and vain, as
to found his *knowledge* upon *ideas*, becaufe our knowledge is *neceffarily* founded
upon them.

When therefore it is faid, *Infinite wifdom can have no commands, but what are
founded on the unalterable reafon of things;*
it might as juftly have been faid, an *infinite Creator* can have no *power* of creating, but what is founded on the *unalterable nature* of creatures.

For the *reafon* of things, is juft as unalterable, as the *nature* of creatures.
And if the reafons and relations of things
be nothing elfe but their *manner* of exiftence,

iftence, or the *ftate* of their nature, certainly the relations of things muft have
the fame *beginning*, and the fame *alter-*
*able* or unalterable nature, as the things
from whence they flow. Unlefs it can
be faid, that a thing may exift in *fuch a*
*manner*, though it does not exift at all.

Nothing is more certain, than that
the relations of things are only the *parti-*
*cular ftate* of their nature, or *manner* of
exiftence; there can therefore, no eternal and unalterable relations exift, but
of things that eternally and unalterably
exift. Unlefs a thing may be faid to
exift eternally and unalterably in fuch
a particular *ftate* of nature, or *manner*
of exiftence, and yet have no eternal
exiftence.

When therefore it is faid again, *The*
*Will of God is always determined by the*
*nature*

*nature and reason of things*—It is the same as if it were said, the *Omnipotence of God* is always determined by the *nature* of *causes* and *effects*. For, as all causes and effects are what they are, and owe their *nature* to the omnipotence of God, so the relations of things are what they are, and owe their nature to the Wisdom and Will of God.

Nor does this dependance of the relations of things on the *Will* of God destroy the nature of relations, or make them doubtful, any more than the existence of things, depending on the *Power* of God, destroys the certainty of their existence, or renders it doubtful. For as God cannot make things to exist, and not to exist at the same time, though their existence depends upon his *Power*, so neither can he make things

to

to have fuch relations, and yet not **to** have fuch relations at the fame time, though their relations depend upon his *Will.*

So that, the afcribing the relations of things to the Will of God, from whence alone they can proceed, brings no uncertainty to thofe duties or rules of life, which flow from fuch relations, but leaves the ftate of nature, with all its relations, and the duties which flow from them, in the greateft certainty, fo long as nature itfelf is continued ; and, when that either *ceafes entirely*, or is only *altered*, it is not to be wondered at, if all its relations ceafe, or are altered with it.—

But, *Dare any one fay, that God's Laws are not founded on the eternal reafon of things?*

I dare fay it, with the fame affurance,

4

as

as that his *Exiflence* is not founded on
the *eternal exiflence* of things. And,
it is the fame extravagance to fay, that
God's laws are founded on the *eternal*
*reafons* of things, as to fay, that his *power*
is founded on the *eternal capacities* of
things. For the *capacities* of things
have juft the fame *folidity* and *eternity*,
as the relations of things have; and
are juft fuch *independent realities* as they
are: and are juft the fame *proper ma-*
*terials* to found the omnipotence of
God upon, as the relations of things are
to found his infinite wifdom upon.

And, as we can fay, that the *Omnipotence*
of God, in preferving and fupporting the
creation, will certainly act *fuitably* to its
felf, and *confiftent* with that omnipotence
which firft made things be what they
are, and put nature into fuch a ftate of
caufes

caufes and effects as it is in; fo we can
fay, that the *infinite Wifdom* of God, in
giving laws to the world, will act *fuitably* to its felf, and *confiftent* with that
wifdom which at firft made the *nature*
and *relations* of the rational world be
what they are.

But then, as the *Omnipotence* of God,
though it acts fuitably to the laws and
ftate of the creation, and the nature of
caufes and effects, which it firft ordain-
ed, yet cannot be faid to be *founded*
upon the nature of caufes and effects; becaufe neither caufes nor effects
have any nature, but what they *owe* to
omnipotence; fo, the infinite *Wifdom* of
God, though in giving laws to the
world, it acts *fuitably* to the natures and
relations of rational beings, yet cannot
be faid to be *founded* upon fuch relations;

tions; becaufe fuch relations are the *effeƈts* of the divine wifdom, and owe their exiftence to it.

And the *reafon* or *relations* of things fhew God's *antecedent* wifdom, and are effeƈts of it, juft as the nature of *caufes* and *effeƈts* fhew his *antecedent* power, and are the effeƈts of it. And as he is infinitely powerful, but not from the *nature* of caufes and effeƈts; fo he is infinitely wife, but not from the *reafon* and *nature* of things.

Again, if God be *infinite* wifdom, then his wifdom cannot be founded on the relations of things; unlefs things *finite*, and relations that began to be, can be the foundation of that wifdom which is infinite, and could not begin to be.

And to afk, What the infinite wifdom of God can be founded upon, if it be not
founded

founded upon the *natures* and *relations* of things, is the fame abfurdity as to afk, How God's wifdom could be *without* a beginning, if we cannot tell *how* it *began?* For if his wifdom be infinite, it can no more be founded upon any thing, or have any reafon of its exiftence, than it can have any thing before it.

Therefore to afk, *what* it is founded upon, when it can have no foundation upon *any thing*, is afking, what an *independent* Being is dependent upon, or *how* that began, which could have *no* beginning?

And to afk the reafon or foundation of *any one* of the divine attributes, is the fame as afking the reafon or foundation of them all. And to feek for the reafon or foundation of *all* the divine attributes,

butes, is feeking for the *Caufe* of God's exiftence.

And as we do not come at God's ex-iftence, till we come to the *end* of *caufes*, fo nothing that is divine, can be attri-buted to any caufe.

Nor is it any more a contradiction to fay, there is fomething whofe nature is without any caufe or foundation of its exiftence, than to fay fomething exifts without ever *beginning* to exift. For as nothing can have a beginning, but as it proceeds from fome caufe; fo that, which can have no beginning, can have no caufe. If therefore the divine wif-dom ever *began* to be *infinite*, and we could know when that beginning was; we fhould have fome pretence to fearch for *that*, upon which its infinity was

*founded;*

*founded;* but if it never could begin to be, then to feek for its reafon, or foundation, is feeking for its beginning.

It may be afked, Is there then no *reafon* or *nature* of things? Yes ; as certainly as there are things. But the nature and reafon of things, confidered *independently* of the divine Will, or *without* it, have no more *obligation* in them, than a *divine worfhip* confidered independently of, and without any regard to the *exiftence* of God. For the *Will* of God is as abfolutely neceffary to found all *moral obligation* upon, as the exiftence of God is neceffary to be the foundation of religious worfhip. And the fitnefs of *moral obligations,* without the *Will* of God, is only like the fitnefs of a *religious* worfhip without the *exiftence* of God.

And

And it is as juft to fay, that he de-
ftroys the *reafon* of religion and piety,
who founds it upon the nature and exiftence of God, as to fay, he faps the
foundation of moral obligations, who
founds them upon the Will of God.
And as religion cannot be juftly or fo-
lidly defended, but by fhewing its con-
nexion with, and dependance upon,
God's exiftence; fo neither can moral
obligations be afferted with ftrength and
reafon, but by fhewing them to be the
Will of God.

It may again be afked, Can God make
that fit in *its felf*, which is in *its felf*
*abfolutely* unfit to be done?

This queftion confifts of improper
terms. For God's Will no more makes
actions to be fit *in themfelves*, than it
makes

makes *things* to exift *in, or of themfelves.*
No things, nor any actions, have any
*abfolute* fitnefs, and in *themfelves.*

A *gift*, a *blow*, the making a *wound*,
or *fhedding* of *blood*, confidered in themfelves, have no *abfolute* fitnefs, but are
fit or unfit according to any variety of
incidental circumftances.

When therefore God, by his Will,
makes any thing fit to be done, he does
not make the thing fit in *its felf*, which
is juft in the *fame ftate* confidered in *its
felf*, as it was before; but, it becomes
fit for the perfon to do it, becaufe he
can only be happy, or do that which is
fit for him to do, by doing the Will of
God.

For inftance, the *bare eating* a fruit,
confidered in *its felf*, is neither fit nor
unfit. If a fruit be appointed by God

I                              for

for our food and nourifhment, then it is
as fit to eat it, as to preferve our lives.
If a fruit be poifonous, then it is as unfit to eat it, as to commit felf-murder.
If eating of a fruit be prohibited by an
exprefs order of God, then it is as unfit to eat it, as to eat our own damna-
tion.

But in none of thefe inftances is the
eating or not eating, confidered in *its
felf, fit* or *unfit*; but has all its fitnefs, or
unfitnefs, from fuch circumftances, as
are entirely owing to the Will of God.

Suppofing, therefore, God to require
a perfon to do fomething, which, according to his prefent circumftances, *without* that command, he ought not to do,
God does not make that which is *abfolutely* unfit in *itfelf*, fit to be done; but
only adds *new circumftances* to an action,

that

that is neither fit nor unfit, moral nor immoral in *itself*, but *because* of its circumstances.

To instance, in the case of *Abraham* required to sacrifice his son. The killing of a man is neither good nor bad, considered *absolutely* in *its self*. It was unlawful for *Abraham* to kill his son, because of the *circumstances* he was in with regard to his son. But when the divine Command was given, *Abraham* was in a *new state;* the action had *new circumstances;* and then it was as lawful for *Abraham* to kill his son, as it was lawful for God to require any man's life, either by *sickness,* or any *other means* he should please to appoint.

And it had been as unlawful for *Abraham* to have disobeyed God in this extraordinary command, as to have

I 2 curfed

curfed God at any *ordinary calamity* of providence.—

Again, it is objected, *If there be nothing right or wrong, good or bad, antecedently and independently of the Will of God, there can be no reason, why God should will, or command one thing, rather than another.*

It is anfwered, *firft*, That all goodnefs, and all poffible perfection, is as *eternal* as God, and as *effential* to him as his exiftence. And to fay, that they are either *antecedent* or *confequent*, *dependent* or *independent* of his Will, would be equally abfurd. To afk, therefore, whether there be not fomething right and wrong, antecedent to the Will of God, to render his Will *capable* of being right, is as abfurd, as to afk for fome antecedent caufe of his exiftence, that

he

he may be proved to exift neceffarily. And to afk, how God can be good, if there be not fomething good independently of him, is afking how he can be infinite, if there be not fomething infinite independently of him. And, to feek for any other *fource* or *reafon* of the divine Goodnefs, befides the divine Nature, is like feeking for fome external caufe, and help of the divine omnipotence.

The goodnefs and wifdom, therefore, by which God is wife and good, and to which all his works of wifdom and goodnefs are owing, are neither *antecedent*, nor *confequent* to his Will.—

*Secondly,* Nothing is more certain, than that all *moral Obligations* and *Duties*, of creatures towards one another, *began* with the exiftence of moral creatures.

4          This

This is as certain, as that all *phyſical
relations,* and corporeal qualities and
effects *began* with the exiſtence of
bodies.

As therefore nothing has the nature
of a cauſe or effect, nothing has any
quality of any kind in bodies, but what
is entirely owing to matter ſo created
and conſtituted by the *Will* of God; ſo,
it is equally certain, that no actions have
any *moral qualities,* but what are wholly
owing to that ſtate and nature in which
they are created by the Will of God.

Moral obligations, therefore, of creatures, have the ſame *origin,* and the *ſame
reaſon,* that natural qualities and effects
have in the corporeal world, *viz. the
ſole Will of God.* And, as in a different
ſtate of matter, bodies would have had
different qualities and effects; ſo, in a

different

different ftate of rational beings, there would be different moral obligations; and nothing could be right or good in their behaviour, but what began then to be right and good, becaufe they then began to exift in fuch a ftate and condition of life. And, as their ftate and condition could have no other caufe or rea fon of its exiftence, but the fole Will of God, fo the caufe and reafon of right and wrong, in fuch a ftate, muft be equally owing to the Will of God.

The pretended *abfolute independent fitneffes*, or *unfitneffes* of actions, therefore, *in themfelves*, are vain *abftractions*, and philofophical *jargon;* ferving no ends of morality; but only helping people to wrangle and difpute away that fincere obedience to God, which is their only happinefs. But, to make thefe imaginary

nary *abfolute fitneſſes* the *common Law* both
of God and man, is ſtill more extravagant. For, if the *circumſtances* of actions, give them their *moral nature,*
ſurely God muſt firſt be in *our* circumſtances, before that, which is a law to
us, can be the ſame law to him.

And, if a father may require that of a
ſon, which his ſon, becauſe of his *different ſtate,* cannot require of his brother;
ſurely that, which God may require of
us, may be as different from that, which
a father may require of a ſon, as God is
different from a father.

To ſay, that the *reaſon* of things is the
ſame law to God as it is to us, is ſay-
ing, that God is in the *ſame ſtate,* with
*regard* to the nature of things, as we
are. For, as things are a law to us, becauſe we are in *ſuch* a ſtate; if they be
the

the *same law* to God, it muſt be, becáuſe God is in the ſame ſtate as we are.

Again, if God be as much under a law as we are, than he is as much under *authority*; for law can no more be without authority, than without a lawgiver. And if God and we are under the *same law*, we muſt be under the *same authority*.

But as God cannot be under any law in common with us, his creatures, any more than he can be of the ſame rank or order with us; ſo neither can he be under any law at all, any more than he can be under any authority at all.

For that, which is the *Rule*, or *Reaſon* of God's actions, is no more different from his own Will, than his power is different from his Will.

And

And though God is not to be looked upon as an *arbitrary Being*, in the fenfe of thofe, who will not diftinguifh arbitrary from *humour* and *caprice*; yet, in a better and only true fenfe of the word, when applied to God, he muft be affirmed to be an arbitrary Being, who acts only *from himfelf*, from his *own Will*, and according to his *own pleafure.*

And we have no more reafon to be afraid to be left to a God without a law, than to a God that had no beginning; or to be left to his Will and pleafure, than to be left under the protection and care of a Being, who is all love, and mercy, and goodnefs. For, as the exiftence of God, as fuch, neceffarily implies the exiftence of all perfection; fo the Will of God, as fuch, neceffarily implies the

*willing*

*willing* every thing, that *all perfection* can will.

And as the exiftence of God, becaufe it contains all perfection, cannot for that reafon have any external Caufe ; fo the Will of God, becaufe it is *all perfection*, cannot, for that reafon, have any external *Rule* or *direction*. But his own Will is Wifdom, and his Wifdom is his Will. His Goodnefs is arbitrary, and his Arbitrarinefs is goodnefs.

To bring God therefore into a ftate of moral obligation and fubjection to any external *Law* or *Rule*, as we are, has all the abfurdity of fuppofing him to be a finite, dependant, temporary; imperfect; improveable, governable Being, as we are.———

The truth of the matter is this ; Reafon is in God and man, as Power is in
God

God and man. And, as the divine *Power* has fome degree of likenefs to human power, yet with an *infinite* diffe- rence from it; fo that perfection, which we call *Reafon* in God, has fome degree of likenefs to reafon as it is in man, yet is *infinitely* and beyond all conception different from it.

Nor can any one fhew, that we enjoy Reafon in a *higher degree* in refpect of God, than we enjoy power; or that the *manner*, or *light* of our Reafon, bears any greater likenefs to the light and knowledge of God, than the *manner* and *extent* of our power bears to the omni- potence of God.

And as our enjoyment of power is fo limited, fo imperfect, fo fuperficial, as to be fcarce fufficient to tell us, what power is, much lefs what omnipotence

is ;

is; fo as our fhare of Reafon is fo fmall, and we enjoy it in fo imperfect a manner, that we can fcarce think or talk intelligibly of it, or fo much as define our own faculties of reafoning.

K

---

## CHAP. II.

*Shewing, from the* ſtate *and* relation *between
God and man, that human Reaſon cannot
poſſibly be a competent judge of the* fitneſs
*and* reaſonableneſs *of God's proceedings
with mankind, either as to the* time, *or*
matter, *or* manner, *of any external Revelation.*

SINCE it has frequently been laid
down as an undeniable Rule of God's
actions, 'that he muſt, if he be a wiſe
and good being, act according to the
relation he ſtands in towards his creatures ; I proceed, *upon this principle,* to
prove the incapacity of *human Reaſon,* to

judge

judge *truly* of God's proceedings in regard to *divine Revelation.*

For, if the fitnefs of actions *refult*
*from the nature and relations* of beings,
.then the *fitnefs* of God's actions, as he is
an *omnifcient Creator* and *Governor*, to whom
every thing is *eternally foreknown*, over
beings endued with *our freedom of will*,
muft be to us very *incomprehenfible.*

We are not fo much as capable of
comprehending, by our own Reafon, the
*poffibility* of this relation, or how the
foreknowledge of God can confift with
the free agency of creatures. We know
that God foreknows all things, with the
fame certainty as we know there is a
God. And, if *felf-confcioufnefs* be an infallible proof of our own exiftence, it
proves, with the fame certainty, the freedom of our will. And hence it is, that
we

we have a full affurance of the confiften-
cy of God's fore-knowledge with freedom of will.

Now this *incomprehenfible* relation between an *eternally fore-knowing Creator*
and *Governor*, and his free creatures, is
the *relation* from whence arifes the *fitnefs*
of God's providence over us. But if
the *relation* itfelf be incomprehenfible,
then thofe actions that have their *fitnefs*
from it, muft furely be incomprehenfible. Nothing can be fit for God to do,
either in *Creation* or *Providence*, but what
has its fitnefs founded in his own *Fore-
knowledge* of every thing that would follow, from *every kind* of creation, and
*every manner* of providence. But if nothing can be fit, but becaufe it is according to *this fore-knowledge* of *every
thing* that would follow, from *every kind*

of

of creation, and *every manner* of providence; then we have the utmoft certainty,
that the *fitnefs* of God's actions, as a *fore-
knowing Creator* and *Governor* of free
agents, muft be founded upon *reafons*,
which we cannot *poffibly* know any thing
of.

And a *Child*, that has but juft learned
to fpeak, is as well qualified to ftate the
fitnefs of the laws of *matter* and *motion*,
by which the whole *vegetable* world is
preferved, as the wifeft of men are qualified to comprehend, or ftate the fitnefs
of the methods, or proceedings, which
a *fore-knowing Providence* preferves over
free agents. For every reafon, on which
*the fitnefs* of fuch a Providence is founded, is not only *unknown* to us, but by a
neceffity of nature *impoffible* to be known
by us.

For

For, if the *fitnefs* of God's acting in this, or that manner, be founded in his *fore-knowledge* of every thing that would *happen*, from *every poffible way* of acting, *then*, it is juft as abfolutely impoffible for us to know the reafons, on which the fitnefs of his actions is founded, as it is impoffible for us to be omnifcient.

What human Reafon can tell, what kind of beings it is *fit* and *reafonable* for God to create, on the account of his own *eternal Fore-knowledge* ? And yet, this is as poffible, as for the fame Reafon to tell, how God ought to govern beings already created, on the account of his own eternal fore-knowledge : and yet, God can neither *create*, nor *govern* his creatures, as it is *fit* and *reafonable* he fhould, unlefs he creates and governs them in *this* or *that* manner, on the *ac-*

*count*

*count* of his own fore-knowledge. And therefore, if he act *like* himfelf, and *worthy* of his own nature, the fitnefs of his proceedings muft for this very reafon, *becaufe* they are fit, be vaftly *above* our comprehenfion.

Who can tell what *different kinds* of rational creatures, diftinguifhed by variety of natures, and faculties, it is fit and reafonable for God to create, becaufe he *eternally forefaw* what would be the *effect* of fuch different creations? Who can explain the *fitnefs* of that vaft *variety* there is amongft rational creatures of the *fame fpecies*, in their rational faculties, or fhew that all their different faculties ought to be as they are? And yet, the *fitnefs* of this providence has its *certain reafon* in the divine fore-knowledge;

ledge; and it could not be fit, but becauſe of it.

Who can tell what *degree* of Reaſon rational creatures ought to enjoy, *becauſe*
they are rational; or what degrees of *new*
and *revealed* knowledge it is fit and reaſonable for God to give, or not give
them, becauſe they ſeem, or ſeem not to
themſelves to want it? are diſpoſed,
or not diſpoſed, to receive it? For, as
mankind cannot tell why it was *fit* and
*reaſonable* for God to create them of ſuch
a *kind*, and *degree*, as they are of; ſo neither can they tell how God ought, or
ought not to add to their natural knowledge, and make them as *differently accountable* for the uſe of revealed rules of
life, as for the uſe of their natural faculties.

And

And as the reason, why God created them of *such* a *kind*, and with *such facul-ties*, was because of his own fore-knowledge of the *effects* of such a creation; so, if ever he do reveal to them any *su-pernatural* knowledge, both *the doing it*, the *time*, and *matter*, and *manner* of it, must have its *fitness* in his own *eternal Fore-knowledge* of the effects of such a Re-velation.

The reasons therefore, on which the *fitness* of this or that Revelation, *why*, or *when*, of *what matter*, in *what manner*, and to *whom* it is to be made, must, from the nature and reason of things, be as un-searchable by us, as the reasons of *this* or *that* creation of rational beings, at such a *time*, of such a *kind*, in such a *state*.

This may help us to an easy solution

of

of thefe *unreasonable* queftions, which are
fo often propofed——

*If the defign of God in communicating any
thing of himfelf to men were their happinefs,
would not that defign have obliged him, who
at all times alike defires their happinefs, to
have at all times alike communicated it to
them? If God always act for the good of his
creatures, what reafon can be affigned, why
he fhould not from the beginning have difcovered fuch things as make for their good, but
defer the doing it, till the time of* Tiberius?
*Since the fooner this was done, the greater
would his goodnefs appear.*

And again, *How is it confiftent with the
notion of God's being univerfally benevolent,
not to have revealed it to all his children, when
all had equal need of it? Was it not as eafy*
                                          *for*

*for him to have communicated it to all nations,
as to any one nation or perfon? Or in all
languages, as in one.*

Now, all this is fully anfwered by one
great and fundamental principle—

*For, if the relations between things and
perfons, and the fitnefs refulting from thence,
be the fole Rule of God's actions ;* then, the
*fole rule* or reafon of God's revealing any
thing to any man, or men, at any time,
muft have its *fitnefs refulting* from the
divine Fore-knowledge of the effects of
*fuch* a revelation, at *fuch* a time, and on
*fuch* perfons. If God do not act thus,
he does not act according to the *relation*
betwixt a *fore-knowing Creator,* and his
free creatures. But if he do act according to a *fitnefs refulting* from this *relation,* and make or do not make revelations, according to his own fore-
knowledge

knowledge of the fitnefs of times, and perfons for them; then, to afk, how a God, *always equally* good, can make a Revelation at *any* time, and not make the *fame* at *all* times, is as abfurd as to afk, how a God, always equally good, can reveal that at one time, becaufe it is a *proper* time for it, and not reveal it at any other time, though every other time is *improper* for it ?

God's goodnefs, directed by his own fore-knowledge of the *fitnefs* of times, and of the *ftate* and *actions* of free agents, deferred a certain Revelation to the time of *Tiberius;* becaufe he *forefaw* it would then be an act of the *greateft* goodnefs, and have its *beft effects* upon the world. To afk therefore, *what reafon can be affigned,* why fo good and beneficial a Revelation was not *fooner,* or even from the

4                                              *begin-*

*beginning* made to the world, is afking,
*What reafon can be affigned*, why God is
good, and intends the *greateft* good by
what does, or ftays for the doing any
thing, till fuch time as makes it a
greater good than if he had done it
fooner; it is afking, why God fhould act
according to his own *fore-knowledge* of
the *ftate* and *actions* of *free agents*, and
order all things according to a fitnefs
refulting from fuch a fore-knowledge?

Now, this appealing to God's Fore-
knowledge of the ftate and actions of
*free agents*, as the Caufe of all that is
particular in the *time* and *manner* of any
revelation, and deducing its fitnefs from
thence, cannot be faid to be *begging the
queftion* in difpute; but is refolving it
directly according to the *Rule*, which is
laid down for God to act by, which is

L this:

this : That *the relations between things and persons, and the fitnefs refulting from thence, muft be the fole rule of God's actions, unlefs he be an arbitrary being.*

But if this be the *fole Rule,* then God in giving any revelation muft act, as the *relation* betwixt a *fore-knowing* Creator and his *free* creatures requires ; and his actions muft have their *fitnefs refulting* from his fore-knowledge of the *ftate* and *actions* of free agents. But if this be God's fole rule, made neceffary to him from the nature of things, then to afk why *this* or *that* revelation was given, *only* at *fuch* a time, is to afk, why God *only* does that which is *fit* for him to do? And to afk, why not the fame revelation at any other time, is afking, why God does not do that, which it is *not fit* for him to do?

But,

But, *Was it not as eafy for God to have communicated it to all nations, as to any one nation or perfon? Or in all languages, as in any one?*—This argument is built upon the *truth* and *reafonablenefs* of this suppofition, That God does things becaufe they are *eafy*, or forbears things becaufe they are *difficult* to be performed. For, it can be no argument, that God ought to have revealed fuch things to *all* nations or perfons, becaufe it was as *eafy* to him, as to do it to *any one* nation or perfon; unlefs it be fuppofed, that the *eafinefs* of a thing is a reafon why God does it, and the difficulty of a thing a reafon why he does not do it. But, if this suppofition be very abfurd, then the argument founded upon it muft be liable to the fame charge.

It is as eafy to God to make all men con-

conformable to his Will, as to make *trees* and *plants* grow according to his plea- fure; but though it is as eafy, yet it is not as *fit* and *reafonable* for God to do all by *power* in the rational world, as he does all by power in the vegetable. It is as eafy for God to deftroy all finful natures, as to preferve them in being; and if he do one rather than the other, it is not becaufe one is *eafier* than the other, but becaufe the perfections of his own nature move him to it.

But if God do things, not becaufe they are eafy, but becaufe they are in- finitely good and fit to be done, and founded in the *relation* of a fore-knowing Creator to his free creatures; then, the reafon why God has afforded different revelations to different ages and perfons is this, That his *manner* of revealing

every

every thing might be *worthy* of his own *fore-knowledge* of the effects of it ; and that every thing, which is particular in the *time* or *manner* of any revelation, might have its *fitness resulting* from the *relation* be-twixt a good God and his creatures, whose *changing* state, *different* conduct, *tempers* and *actions* are all eternally fore-known by him.

Again; it is objected, that a divine Revelation must either be the effect of *Justice,* or else of *Mercy* and *free Goodness*; but in either of these cases it ought to be *universal;* for justice must be done to all. But, if it be the effect of *mercy* and *free goodness,* it is asked, *How a being can be denominated merciful and good, who is so only to a few, but cruel and unmerciful to the rest ?*

It is answered, That there is neither

*Justice*

*Juſtice* in God without Mercy, nor *Mer-cy*, without Juſtice; and to aſcribe a *Re-velation* to either of them ſeparately, in *contradiſtinction* to the other, has no more truth or reaſon in it, than to aſcribe the *Creation* ſeparately either to the *Wiſ-dom*, or *Power* of God, in contradiſtinc-tion to the other.

*Secondly,* ☞ A divine revelation is not owing to the *juſtice* or *free goodneſs* of God, either *ſeparately* or *jointly* con-ſidered; but to the goodneſs, mercy, and juſtice of God, *governed* and *directed* by his eternal Fore-knowledge of all the effects of every revelation, at any, or all times.

God ordains a Revelation in this or that manner, time, and place; not be-cauſe it is a *juſtice* that he cannot refuſe, nor

nor becaufe it is matter of *favour* or *free* Goodnefs, and therefore may be given in any manner at pleafure ; but becaufe he has the whole *duration* of human things, the whole *race* of mankind, the whole *order* of human changes and events, the whole *combination* of all caufes and effects of human tempers, all the *actions* of free agents, and *all the confequences* of every revelation plainly in his fight ; and according to this eternal *Fore-knowledge*, every revelation receives every thing that is *particular* in it, either as to *time, matter, manner,* or *place*.

All complaints therefore, about that which is *particular* or *feemingly* partial in the time and manner of any revelation, are very unjuftifiable ; and fhew, that we are difcontent at God's proceedings, becaufe

becaufe he acts like himfelf, does what is *beft* and *fitteft* to be done, and governs the world, not according to our weak imaginations, but according to his own infinite perfections.

We will not allow a Providence to be *right*, unlefs we can comprehend and explain the reafonablenefs of all its fteps ; and yet it could not *poffibly* be right, unlefs its proceedings were as much *above* our comprehenfion, as our wifdom is *below* that which is infinite.

For, if the *relations* of *things* and *perfons*, and the *fitnefs* refulting from thence, be the *Rule* of God's actions ; then, all the revelations that come from God, muft have their *fitnefs* refulting from the relation his Fore-knowledge bears to the *various ftates, conditions, tempers,* and *actions* of free agents, and the

*various*

*various effects* of every manner of revelation.

But, if God cannot act worthy of himfelf, in any manner of revelation, unlefs
he acts according to a fitnefs refulting
from this relation; then, we have the
higheft certainty, that he muft act by a
*Rule* that lies *out of our fight;* and that
his Providence in this particular muft be
*incomprehenfible* to us, for this very reafon, becaufe it has that very fitnefs, wifdom, and goodnefs in it, which it ought
to have.

---

### CHAP. III.

*Shewing, how far human Reason is ena-
bled to judge of the* reasonableness,
truth, *and* certainty *of divine* Revelation.

THE former chapter has plainly
shewn, from the state and relation between God and man, that we must be
strangers to the true reasons on which a
divine Revelation is founded, both as to
its *time, matter,* and *manner.*

But it is here objected, *If God, by reason of his own perfections, must be thus my-
sterious and incomprehensible, both in the
matter and manner of divine Revelation;*

*how*

*how can we know what revelations we are to receive as divine? How can we be blamed for rejecting this, or receiving that, if we cannot comprehend the reasons on which every Revelation is founded, both as to its matter and manner?*

Juſt as we may be blamed for ſome notions of God, and commended for others, though we can have no notions of God, but ſuch as are *myſterious* and *inconceivable*. We are not without ſome natural capacity of judging right of God, of finding out his perfections, and prov-ing what is or is not worthy to be aſcribed to him. Yet, what the divine perfections are in themſelves, what they imply and contain in their own nature and manner of exiſtence, is altogether myſterious and inconceivable by us, at preſent. If therefore a man may be

blameable

blameable or commendable for his right
or wrong belief of a God; then a man
may be accountable for a right or wrong
belief of fuch matters, as are in their own
nature too myfterious for his comprehenfion. And, though a man knows the reafons of a divine Revelation, either as to
its *matter* or *manner*, as imperfectly as he
knows the divine nature; yet he may be
as liable to account for believing *falfe
revelations*, as for *idolatry;* and as full of
guilt for rejecting a *true Revelation*, as for
denying the only *true God*.

*Secondly,* Though we are infuffi-
cient for comprehending the *reafons*, on
which the particular *matter* or *manner* of
any divine Revelation is founded; yet
we may be fo far fufficient judges of the
*reafons* for *receiving* or not *receiving* a revelation

velation as divine, as to make our conduct therein juftly accountable to God.

For, if God can fhew a Revelation to
proceed from him by the *fame undeniable*
evidence, as he fhews the *Creation* to be
his *work;* if he can make himfelf as vifible in a *particular extraordinary* manner,
as he is by his *general* and *ordinary* Providence, then, though we are as unqualified
to judge of the myfteries of a *Revelation,*
as we are to judge of the myfteries in
*Creation* and *Providence*; yet, we may be
as fully obliged to receive a Revelation,
as to acknowledge the Creation to be the
work of God; and as highly criminal
for difbelieving it, as for denying a general Providence.

*Adam, Noah, Abraham,* and *Mofes* were
very incompetent judges of the reafons
on which the particular Revelations

made

made to them were founded; but this did not hinder their fufficient affurance, that fuch Revelations came from God; becaufe, they were proved to come from God in the fame manner, and for the fame reafons, as the Creation is proved to be the Work of God.

And as *Adam* and *Noah* muft fee every thing *wonderful, myfterious,* and *above their comprehenfions* in thofe new worlds, into which they were introduced by God; fo they could no more expect that he fhould require nothing of them, but what they would enjoin themfelves, than that their own *frame,* the *nature* of the creation, the *providence* of God, or the *ftate* of human life, fhould be exactly as they would have it.

And if their pofterity will let no *mef-fages* from heaven, no *prophecies* and *mi-racles*

*racles* perfuade them, that God can call them to any duties, but fuch as they muft enjoin themfelves; or to the belief of any doctrines, but fuch as their own minds can fuggeft; nor to any methods of changing their prefent ftate of weaknefs. and diforder for a happy immortality but fuch as fuit their own *tafte, temper,* and *way of reafoning;*. it is, becaufe they are grown fenfelefs of *the myfteries of creation* and *providence*, with which they are furrounded, and forget the awful prerogative of *infinite wifdom* over the weakeft, loweft rank of intelligent beings.

For the *Excellence* of a Revelation is to be acknowledged by us, for the fame reafon that we are to acknowledge the excellence of Creation and Providence; not becaufe they are wholly according to human conception, and have no my-

fteries,

fleries, but becaufe they are proved to be of God.

And a Revelation is to be received as coming from God, not becaufe of its internal excellence, or becaufe we judge it to be worthy of God; but becaufe God has declared it to be his, in as *plain* and *undeniable* a manner, as he has declared *Creation* and *Providence* to be his. For, though no Revelation can come from God, but what is truly worthy of him, and full of every internal excellence; yet, what is truly *worthy* of God to be *revealed*, cannot poffibly be known by us, but by a Revelation from himfelf.

And, as we can only know what is worthy of God in Creation, by knowing what he has created; fo we can no other way poffibly know what is worthy of God to be revealed, but by a Revelation.

tion. And he that pretends, independently of any Revelation, to fhew *how*, and in what manner God ought to make a Revelation worthy of himfelf, is as great a *Vifionary*, as he that fhould pretend, independently of the Creation, or without learning any thing from it, to fhew how God ought to have proceeded in it, to make it worthy of himfelf. For, as God alone knows how to create worthy of himfelf, and nothing can poffibly be proved to be worthy to be created by him, but becaufe he has already created it ; fo God alone knows what is worthy of himfelf in a Revelation, and nothing can poffibly be proved worthy to be revealed by him, but becaufe he has already revealed it.

Were it allowed that a Revelation cannot be divine, if it contain any thing

*myfte-*

*myfterious,* whofe fitnefs and neceffity cannot be explained by human Reafon, then neither *Creation* nor *Providence* can be proved to be divine; for they are both of them *more myfterious* than the Chriftian revelation. And Revelation itfelf is *therefore* myfterious, becaufe Creation and Providence cannot be delivered from myftery. And, were it poffible for man to comprehend the reafons, on which the *manner* of the Creation and divine Providence are founded, then Revelation might be without myfteries.

But, if the *Myfteries* in Revelation be owing to that, which is, by the nature of things incomprehenfible in Creation and Providence, then, it is very *unreafonable* to reject Revelation, becaufe it has that which it muft neceffarily have; not from itfelf, but from the nature and ftate of
things

things. And much worfe is it to deny Revelation to be divine, for fuch a reafon, as makes it equally fit to deny *Creation* and *Providence* to be of God.

For, if every thing be *arbitrary*, whofe *fitnefs and expedience* human Reafon cannot *prove* and *explain*, then furely an *invifible over-ruling Providence*, that orders all things in a manner, and for reafons known only to its felf; that fubjects human life, and human affairs to what changes it pleafes; that confounds the beft laid defigns, and makes great effects arife from folly and imprudence; that gives the race not to the fwift, nor the battle to the ftrong; that brings good men into affliction, and makes the wicked profperous; furely *fuch a Providence* muft be highly arbitrary.

And, therefore, if this argument be to

be

be admitted, it leads directly to *Atheism*, and brings us under a greater neceffity of rejecting this notion of divine Providence, on the account of its *myfteries*, than of rejecting a Revelation that is myfterious in any of its doctrines. And if God cannot be faid to deal with us as rational agent, if he requires any thing of us, that *our Reafon* cannot prove to be neceffary, furely he cannot be faid to deal with us as rational and moral agents, if he over-rule our perfons and affairs, and difappoint our counfels ; make weaknefs profperous, and wifdom unfucceffful, in a *fecret* and *invifible* manner, and for reafons and ends that we have no means of knowing.

And, if it may be faid, To what purpofe has he given us Reafon, if that be not folely to give laws to us ? furely it

may

may better be faid, To what purpofe has
he given us Reafon to take care of ourfelves, to provide for our happinefs, to
prepare *proper* means for certain ends,
if there be *an over-ruling Providence*, that
changes the *natural courfe* of things ; that
confounds the beft laid defigns; and dif-
appoints the wifeft counfels ?

☞ There is nothing therefore *half
fo myfterious* in *the Chriftian revelation,*
confidered in itfelf, as there is in that
*invifible Providence,* which all muft hold,
who believe a God.  And though there
is enough plain in Providence, to excite
the admiration of humble and pious
minds, yet it has often been a rock of
*Atheifm* to thofe, who make *their own
Reafon* the meafure of wifdom.

Again, Though the *Creation* plainly de-
clares the glory, and wifdom, and goodnefs

nefs of God ; yet it has *more myfteries in* it, more things whofe fitnefs, expedience, and reafonablenefs, human Reafon cannot comprehend, than are to be found in Scripture.

If therefore he reafon right, who fays, *If there may be fome things in a true Religion, whofe fitnefs and expedience we cannot fee, why not others ? Nay, why not the whole? fince that would make God's laws all of a piece. And, if the having of thefe things be no proof of its falfhood, how can any things fit and expedient [which no Religion is without] be a proof of the truth of any one Religion ?* If I fay, this be right reafoning, then it may be faid, *If there be things in the Creation, whofe fitnefs we cannot fee, why not others ? Nay, why not the whole? fince that would make all God's works of a piece. And if the being of fuch things as*
                                                    *thefe*

*these in the Creation be not a proof of its*
*not being divine, how can the fitness and*
*expedience of any Creation prove, that it*
*is the work of God?*

. Thus does this argument tend wholly
to Atheifm, and concludes with the
fame force againft *Creation* and *Provi-*
*dence*, as it does againft Revelation.

The true grounds and reafons, on which
we are to believe a Revelation to be divine, are fuch external marks and figns
of God's action and operation, as are a
fufficient proof of it. And if God have
no ways of acting that are peculiar and
particular to himfelf, and fuch as fufficiently prove his action and operation,
then Revelation can have no . fufficient
proof that it comes from God.

And if a Revelation had no other
proof of its Divinity, but fuch an in-

ternal

ternal excellency and fitnefs of its doctrines, as is fully known and approved
by *human Reafon;* fuch an internal excellency would be fo far from being a
fufficient proof of its Divinity, that it
would be a probable objection againft it.
For it has an appearance of great proba-
bility, that God would not make an external Revelation of that *only,* which
was *fufficiently* and fully known without it.

Although, therefore, no Revelation can
come from God, whofe doctrines have
not an *internal excellency,* and the *higheft
fitnefs;* yet the non-appearance of fuch
excellency and fitnefs to *our Reafon,* cannot be a difproof of its Divinity; becaufe, it is our ignorance of fuch matters,
without Revelation, which is the *true
ground and reafon* of God's revealing any
thing to us.

The

The Credibility, therefore, of divine Revelation refts chiefly upon *fuch exter-nal* evidence, as is a fufficient proof of the divine operation, or interpofition. If there be no fuch external evidence pof-fible; if God has no ways of acting fo *peculiar* to himfelf, as to be a *fufficient* proof of his action, then a Revelation cannot be fufficiently proved to be divine.

I appeal therefore to the *Miracles* and *Prophecies,* on which Chriftianity is founded, as a *fufficient* proof it is a divine Revelation. And fhall here confider, what is objected againft the fufficiency of this kind of proof.

1. It is objected, That Miracles can-not prove a *falfe,* or *bad* doctrine, to be *true* and *good;* therefore miracles, *as fuch,* cannot prove the truth of any Revelation.

N    But

But, though miracles cannot prove falfe to be true, or bad to be good; yet they may prove, that we ought to 're-ceive fuch doctrines, both as true and good, which we could not know to be true and good without fuch miracles.

Not becaufe the miracles have any influence upon the things revealed, but becaufe they teftify the credibility of the Revealer, as having God's teftimony to the truth of that which he reveals.

If therefore miracles can be a fuffici-ent proof of God's fending any perfons to fpeak in his name, and under his authority ; then they may be a fufficient proof of the truth and divinity of a Re-velation, though they cannot prove that which is falfe to be true.

But, *If evil beings can imprefs notions in men's minds as ftrongly as good beings, and*

3                                      *caufe*

*cause miracles to be done in confirmation of them; is there any way to know to which of the two notions, thus impressed, are owing, but from their nature and tendency, or internal marks of wisdom and goodness?——— And if so, Can external proofs carry us any farther than the internal proofs do?*

This objection supposes, that no miracles, *as such*, can be a sufficient proof of the divinity of a revelation; for this reason, because we do not know the extent of that power, which evil spirits have, of doing miracles. But this objection is groundless. For, granting that we do not know the nature and extent of that power which evil spirits may have; yet, if we know *enough* of it to affirm, that the *Creation* is not the work of evil spirits; if we can securely appeal to the Creation, as a *sufficient proof* of God's action

action and operation; then we are fully secure in appealing to miracles, as a sufficient proof of a divine revelation.

For, if the Creation must of necessity be allowed to be the work of God, notwithstanding any *unknown degree* of power in evil spirits; if we can as certainly ascribe it to God, as if we really knew there were no *such* spirits; then miracles may be as full a proof of the operation, or interposition of God, as if we really knew there were no such spirits in being.

I do not ask, Whether the *same divine* perfection is necessary to foretel such things as are foretold in Scripture, and work such miracles as are there related, as is necessary to *create*. I do not ask, Whether any power less than divine can do such things? I only ask, Whether
there

there be any certainty, that the Creation
is the work of God? Whether we can
be fure of the divine operation, from the
exiftence of that creation, which we are
acquainted with? Or, Whether we are
in any *doubt* or *uncertainty* about it, becaufe we do not know the *true nature* or
*degree* of power, that may belong to
evil fpirits?

For, if it can be affirmed with certainty, that the Creation is the work of God,
notwithftanding our uncertainty about
the degree of power that may belong to
evil fpirits; then we have the fame certainty, that the *Prophecies* and *Miracles*
recorded in Scripture are to be afcribed
to God, as his doing, notwithftanding
our uncertainty of the power of evil
fpirits.

And this is affirmed, not becaufe *Prophecies*

*phecies* and *Miracles* require the *same de-gree* of divine power, as to create *ex nihi-lo,* [for that would be affirming we know not what] but it is affirmed, becaufe the Creation cannot be a *better, farther,* or *different* proof of the action or operation of God, than fuch miracles and prophe-cies are.

For, every reafon for afcribing the creation to God, is the fame reafon for afcribing fuch miracles and prophe-cies to God; and every argument againft the certainty of thofe miracles and pro-phecies coming from God, is the fame argument againft the certainty of the Creation's being the work of God; for there cannot be more or lefs certainty in one cafe than in the other.

For, if evil fpirits have fo the creation in their hands, that by reafon of their

power

power over it, *no miracles* can prove the operation of God, then the operation of God cannot be proved from the Creation itfelf.

• For the Creation cannot be proved to be the operation of God, unlefs it can be proved that God *ftill prefides* over it.

And if *all* that, which is extraordinary and miraculous, may be accounted for without the interpofition of God; then nothing that is ordinary and common, according to the courfe of nature, can be a proof of the action of God. For there can be no reafon affigned, why that which is *ordinary* fhould be afcribed to God, if all that is, or has, or can be *miraculous*, may be afcribed to evil fpirits.

Either therefore it muft be faid, that there are or may be miracles, which can-

not

not be the effects of evil fpirits; or elfe, nothing that is ordinary and common can be a proof of the operation of God. For, if nothing miraculous can be an un-deniable proof of God's action, nothing created can be a proof of it.

The matter, therefore, ftands thus: There are, and may be, Miracles, that cannot be afcribed to evil fpirits, with-out afcribing the Creation to them; and which can no more be doubted to come from God, than we can doubt of his be-ing the Creator of the world. There may be miracles therefore, which, *as fuch*, and, confidered *in themfelves*, are as full a proof of the *truth* of that which they atteft, as the Creation is of the *fit-nefs* of that which is created.

And though the *matter* of a Revela-tion is to be attended to, that we may
fully

fully underſtand it, and be rightly af-
fected with it; yet the reaſon of our receiving it as divine, muſt reſt upon that
*external authority*, which ſhews it to be
of God.

And the authority of Miracles, ſufficiently plain and apparent, are of themſelves a full and neceſſary reaſon for receiving a Revelation, which, both as to
its *matter* and *manner*, would not be approved by us without them.

It ſeems therefore, to be a *needleſs*, and
too *great* a conceſſion, which ſome *learned
divines* make in this matter, when they
grant, that we muſt firſt examine the
Doctrines revealed by Miracles, and ſee
whether they contain any thing in them
*abſurd*, or *unworthy* of God, before we
can receive the Miracles as divine. For,

1. Where

1. Where there can be nothing doubt-ed, nor any more required, to make the Miracles fufficiently plain and evident, there can be no doubt about the truth and goodnefs of the Doctrine they atteft. Miracles, in fuch a ftate as this, are the laft refort; they determine for them-felves, and cannot be tried by any thing farther.

And as the *exiftence* of things is the higheft and utmoft evidence of God's having created them, and is not to be tried by *our judgments* about the reafona-blenefs and ends of their creation; fo a courfe of plain undeniable Miracles, at-tefting the truth of a Revelation, is the *higheft* and *utmoft* evidence of its coming from God, and is not to be tried by our judgments about the *reafonablenefs* or *ne-ceffity* of its doctrines.

And

And this is to be affirmed, not becaufe God is too good to fuffer us to be brought into fuch a fnare, but becaufe we can know nothing of God, if fuch a courfe of Miracles be not a fufficient proof of his action and interpofition. For if Doctrines, revealed by fuch an *undeniable change* in the natural courfe of things, have not thence a fufficient proof, that they are divine doctrines ; then *no Laws*, that are according to the natural ftate of things, can have *thence* any proof, that they are *divine laws*.

For if *no courfe* of *miracles* can be of *its felf* a fufficient proof, that *that* which is attefted by them, is attefted by God; then no *fettled, ordinary* ftate of things can of *its felf* be a proof, that *that* which is required by the natural ftate of things, is required by God.

2. To

2. To try Miracles, fufficiently plain and evident, by *our judgments* of the reafonablenefs of the doctrines revealed by them, feems to be beginning at the wrong end. For the Doctrines had not been revealed, but becaufe of our ignorance of the *nature* and *reafonablenefs* of them; nor had the Miracles been wrought, but to *prevent* our *acquiefcing* in our own judgments about the worth and value of them.

3. To fay, That no Miracles, however plain and evident, are to be received as divine, if they atteft any Doctrine that appears to *human Reafon* to be abfurd, or unworthy of God, is very unreafonable. For what is it that can be called *human Reafon* in this refpect? Is it any thing elfe than human opinion? And is

there

there any thing that mankind are in
greater uncertainty, or more contrary to
one another, than in their opinions about
what is abfurd, or unworthy of God in
religion ? And is it not the very end and
defign of a divine Revelation, to help us
to a Rule that may put an end to the di-
vifions of human Reafon, and furnifh us
with an authority for believing fuch
things, as we fhould not think it reafonable to believe without it.

And how weak and ufelefs muft that
Revelation be, which has not fufficient
authority to teach us *new notions* of religion, and perfuade us to believe that to
be reafonable and worthy of God, which
we could not believe to be fo upon a lefs
authority.

But if this be the cafe, as it feems
clearly to be, then we are not to try plain

and evident Miracles of the higheft kind, by *our judgments* of the reafonablenefs of the doctrines revealed by them ; but Miracles are to be received, as of fufficient authority to form and govern our opinions about the reafonablenefs of the doctrines.

It may perhaps be faid, though the authority of Miracles is fufficient to govern our opinions in doctrines that are only myfterious, and above the comprehenfion of our Reafon, yet that which is plainly and grofly abfurd, or unworthy of God, cannot, nor ought to be received upon any authority of the greateft Miracles.

This objection is vain and abfurd ; it is vain, becaufe it relates to a cafe, that never was the cafe of Miracles ; and it is abfurd, becaufe it is providing againft a

cafe

cafe that never can happen to Miracles. For to fuppofe any thing in its own nature grofly abfurd, or unworthy of God, to be attefted with the higheft evidence of miracles, is as impoffible and contradictory a fuppofition, as to fuppofe God to create rational beings wicked in their nature, that they might thereby be of fervice to the devil. Thefe two fuppofitions have not the fmalleft difference, either in abfurdity, or impoffibility.

Again, The hiftory of magical wonders, and extraordinary things done by evil fpirits, is no objection againft the fufficiency of that proof that arifes from Miracles. For, the queftion is not, whether nothing that is extraordinary can be done by evil fpirits, in any circumftances, but whether nothing that is miraculous

miraculous can, as such, be a proof of its being done by God. For these two cases are very consistent; it may be very possible for evil spirits to do things extraordinary in some circumstances, as where people enter into contracts with them, and resign themselves up to their power, and yet that Miracles may, in *other circumstances*, merely as Miracles, be a sufficient proof of their being done by God.

Thus the case of the *Egyptian magicians*, is so far from abating the weight of miracles, that it is a great proof of their authority, considered in themselves. For the *Magicians* could proceed but a little way in their contention with *Moses*; they were soon made to feel his superior power in the same manner, as the rest of the *Egyptians* did, and to confess that his Miracles were done by the *Finger of God.*

*God.* This very inftance therefore fully
fhews, that Miracles, *as fuch,* may be a
fufficient proof of God's interpofition.
For if, in the cafe of a contention, the
fuperior power muft be afcribed to God,
then Miracles as *fuch,* or of *fuch a kind,*
as having none equal to them, or able
to ftand againft them, muft, in fuch a
ftate, be a fufficient proof of their being
done by God, and give a fufficient war-
rant to receive any Doctrine that is attefted by them.

For, let it be fuppofed, that the *Egyptian* Magicians had deftroyed the power
of *Mofes,* and brought all the *miraculous
evils* upon the *Ifraelites,* as enemies of the
*Egyptian* Gods, which he brought upon
them ; what confequence muft *Reafon*
have drawn from fuch an event ? Could
*Reafon* have proved, that the God that
made

made the world was *one* God, and that he alone ought to be worshipped? Or that the *Egyptians* ought to have left their Gods, who had the *whole Creation* in their hands in such a manner, as to change the nature of things as they pleased, and destroy every power that opposed them.

Now, either the case here supposed is possible, or it is impossible. If it be possible, then all the reasons for worshipping the *one true God*, taken from the *nature* and *state* of the creation, may entirely cease, and be so many reasons for idolatrous worship. For no one can have any reasons for worshipping the one true God, from the nature and state of the Creation, if other Gods have the greatest power over it, and can turn every thing into a *plague* upon those that do not worship them.

But

But if this cafe be impoffible, then it
neceffarily follows, that Miracles, *as fuch*,
and confidered *in themfelves*, may be certain and infallible proofs of God's interpofition. For this cafe can only be impoffible, becaufe the greateft, plaineft
Miracles cannot poffibly be on the fide
of error. But if this cannot be, then the
greateft, plaineft Miracles, *as fuch*, and
confidered *in themfelves*, are an infallible
mark of truth.

And he that abides by Miracles in fuch
circumftances, as proofs of the operation
of the *one true* God, has the fame certainty of proceeding right, as he that
takes the ftate and nature of the Creation to be the effect of the one true
God.

And as Miracles, thus confidered in
themfelves, are the higheft and moft
undeniable

undeniable evidence of the truth and divinity of any Revelation; fo Chriftianity ftands fully diftinguifhed from all other religions, by the higheft and moft undeniable evidence; fince it has all the proof that the *higheft ftate* of Miracles can give, and every other religion is without any fupport from them.

Thus I have, from a confideration of the ftate and condition of man, and the feveral relations which God ftands in towards his creatures, fhewn, that it is utterly impoffible for human Reafon to be a competent judge of the fitnefs, or unfitnefs, of all that God may, or may not, require of us. The two following chapters fhall ftate the nature and perfection of Reafon, confidered in itfelf, or as it is a faculty, or principle of action in human nature.

CHAP.

---

## CHAP. IV.

*Of the state and nature of REASON, as
it is in man; and how its perfection in
matters of Religion is to be known.*

PEOPLE, who take to themselves the
names of *Free-thinkers*, make their court
to the world, by pretending to vindicate
the right that all men have, to judge and
act according to their own Reason.
Though, I think, the world have no more
to thank them for on this account, than
if they had pretended to assert the right
that every man has, to see *only* with his
own *eyes*, or to hear *only* with his *own*,
*ears*.

For

For their own Reafon always did, does, and ever will, govern rational creatures, in every thing they determine, either in fpeculation or practice. It is not a matter of *duty* for men to ufe their own Reafon, but of *neceffity:* and it is as impoffible to do otherwife, as for a Being, that cannot act but from choice, to act without choice. And if a man were to try not to act according to his own Reafon or Choice, he would find himfelf under the fame difficulty, as he that tries to think, without thinking upon fomething.

And if God were to command us, by frefh revelations, every day of our lives, not to act from a principle of Reafon and Choice, fuch revelations could have no more effect upon us, than if they came from the weakeft amongft mankind. For, as our principle of acting is

not

not derived from ourfelves, fo it is no
more in our power to alter it, or con-
tradict it, than it is in the power of matter not to *gravitate*, or to exift, without
taking up fome *place*.

Man is under the fame neceffity of
acting from his own choice, that *matter*
is of not acting at all: and a being,
whofe principle of action is Reafon and
Choice, can no more act without it, or
contrary to it, than an extended being
can be without extenfion.

All men, therefore, are equally reafonable in this refpect, that they are, and
muft be, by a *neceffity* of nature, equally
directed and governed by their own
Reafon and Choice.

For, as the principle of action, in human nature, is *Reafon* and *Choice*, and
nothing can be done, or believed, but for

2

*fome*

*fome reafon,* any more than a thing can be chofen and not be chofen ; fo the acting according to one's own Reafon, is not the privilege of the *Philofopher,* but ef-fential to human nature ; and as infe-parable from all perfons, as felf-con-fcioufnefs, or a fenfe of their own ex-iftence.

The difpute, therefore, betwixt *Chrif-tians* and *Unbelievers,* concerning Reafon, is not, whether men are to ufe their *own Reafon,* any more, than whether they are to fee with their *own eyes* ; but whether every man's Reafon muft needs guide him by its *own light,* or muft ceafe to guide him, as foon as it guides him by a light borrowed from Revelation ? This is the true ftate of the queftion ; not *whether* Reafon is to be followed, but when it is *beft* followed ? not whether it

is

is to be our *Guide,* but how it may be made our *safest guide.*

The *Free-thinkers,* therefore, rather appeal to the Paſſions, than the Reaſon of the people, when they repreſent the Clergy and Chriſtianity as enemies to Reaſon, and juſt thinking, and themſelves as friends and advocates for the uſe of Reaſon.

For, Chriſtians pretend to no guide, but under the guidance of their Reaſon; nor to aſſert any thing, but becauſe it cannot be reaſonably denied. They oppoſe unbelievers, not becauſe they *reaſon,* but becauſe reaſon *ill.* They receive Revelation, not to ſuppreſs the power, but to improve the light of their Reaſon; not to take away their right of judging for themſelves, but to ſecure them from falſe Judgments: and what-

P ever

ever is required to be believed, or prac-
tifed, by Revelation, is only fo far required, as there is reafon for it; or, becaufe it is more reafonable than the
contrary.

If, therefore, a poor peafant fhould
call upon our Free-thinkers, to lay afide
their *bigotry* to *ideas, arguments,* and *philofophy,* and govern themfelves by Reafon ; it would be no more abfurd, than
for them to exhort Chriftians to lay
afide their bigotry to *creeds* and *doctrines*
of Revelation, and to govern themfelves
by Reafon.

For it may as well be affirmed, that a
man departs from the ufe of his Reafon,
becaufe he depends upon *ideas, arguments,* and *fyllogifms ;* as that he departs
from the ufe of his Reafon, becaufe he
proceeds

proceeds upon *Prophecies, Miracles,* and *Revelations.*

And if he use his Reason weakly, and be subject to delusion in these points, he no more renounces his Reason, or goes over to another direction, than *Hobbes, Spinosa, Bayle, Collins,* or *Toland,* renounce their Reason, when they take their own *fancies* to be demonstrations.

Christians, therefore, do not differ from unbelievers, in the constant use of their Reason, but in *the manner* of using it: as *virtuous* men differ from *Rakes,* not in their desire of happiness, but in their manner of seeking it.

It appears from what has been said, that, Every man's own Reason is his only principle of action; and that he must judge according to it, whether he receives, or rejects, Revelation.

Now,

Now, although every man is to judge
according to the light of his own Reafon, yet his Reafon has very little light
that can be called *its own*. For, as we
derive our nature from our parents, fo
that which we call generally *natural
knowledge*, or the light of *nature*, is a
knowledge and light that is made natural to us, by the *fame authority* which
makes a certain *language*, certain *cuftoms*,
and *modes* of behaviour, natural to us.

Nothing feems to be our own, but a
*bare capacity* to be inftructed, a nature
*fitted* for any impreffions; as capable of
vice as virtue; as ready to be made a
vicious animal, as a religious rational
creature; as liable to be made a *Hotten-
tot*, by being born among Hottentots,
as to be a *Chriftian*, by being born among
Chriftians.

So

So that our moral and religious knowledge is not to be imputed to the internal light of our *own Reafon* and *Nature*,
but to the happinefs of having been
born amongft reafonable beings, who
have made a fenfe of religion and morality as natural to our minds, as *articulate language* to our tongues.

It is not my intention by this, to fignify that there is not a *good* and *evil*, *right*
and *wrong*, founded in the nature of
things ; or that morality has any dependance upon the *opinions* or *cuftoms* of
men ; but only to fhew, that we *find* out
this right and wrong, come to a *fenfe* of
this good and evil, not by any inward
ftrength, or light, that nature of itfelf
affords, but by fuch *external means*, as
people are taught *articulate* language;

*civility,*

*civility, politenefs,* or any other *rules* of civil life.

Men do not prefer virtue to vice, from a philofophical contemplation of the fit-nefs of the one, and the unfitnefs of the other, founded in the nature of things; but becaufe it is a judgment as *early* in their minds, as their knowledge of the words, Virtue and Vice.

And it can no more be reafonably af-firmed, that our knowledge of God and divine things, our opinions in morality, of the excellency of this or that virtue, of the immortality of our fouls, of a fu-ture life, of rewards and punifhments, are the effects of our natural light; than it can be reafonably affirmed, that our liv-ing in *fociety,* our *articulate* language, and *erect pofture,* are owing to the light of nature.

For,

For, as all mankind find themselves in this state, before any reasoning about it; as *education*, and *human authority* have set our bodies *upright*, taught us *language*, and accustomed us to the *rules* and *manners* of a social life; so *education*, and the *same human* authority, have impressed and planted in our minds, certain notions of God and divine things, and formed us to a sense of good and evil, a belief of our soul's immortality, and the expectation of another life.

And mankind are no more left to find out a God, or the fitness of moral virtue, by their own Reason, than they are left by their own Reason to find out who are their parents, or to find out the fitness of speaking an articulate language, or the reasonableness of living in society.

On the contrary; we know that our

manner

manner of coming into the world 'fubjects us, without any choice, to the *language*, *jentiments, opinions,* and *manners* of thofe amongft whom we are born. And though, when we come to any ftrength, or art of reafoning, or have a *genius* for philofophick enquires, we may thence deduce proofs of the *Being* and *Attributes* of God, the *Reafonablenefs* of religion and morality, the *Nature* of our fouls, and the *Certainty* of a future ftate, and find that the opinions and tradition of mankind, concerning thefe things, are well founded; yet thefe are an *after-knowledge,* not common to men, but accidental confirmations of that know-ledge and belief of a God, Religion, and Morality, which were before fixed in us more or lefs, by education, and the

2                                authority

authority of thofe amongft whom we
have lived.

And as no *Philofopher* ever proved the
*fitnefs* of human nature for a *focial* life,
from principles of reafon and fpeculation,
who had not *firft* been taught the nature
and advantage of Society *another way;* fo
no one ever pretended to prove the Being and attributes of God, or the excellency of moral Virtue, who had not *firft*
been taught the knowledge of God and
moral virtue fome *other way.*

Now, if this be the ftate of Reafon, as
it is in man ; if this be all the light that
we have from our *own nature,* a *bare capacity* of receiving good or bad impreffions, right or wrong opinions and fentiments, according to the ftate of the world
that we fall into ; then we are but poorly
furnifhed

furnifhed, to affert and maintain the *ab-folute perfection* of our own Reafon.

If our light be little more than the opinions and cuftoms of thofe amongft whom we live; and it be fo hard for a man to arrive at a greater wifdom, than the common wifdom of the *place* or *country* which gave him birth and education; how unreafonably do we appeal to the perfection and fufficiency of our own Reafon, againft the *neceffity* and *advantage* of divine Revelation?

If we be *nothing* without the affiftance of men; if we be a kind of foolifh, helplefs animals, till education and experience have *revealed* to us the wifdom and knowledge of our fellow-creatures; fhall we think ourfelves too wife, and full of our own light, to be farther enlightened.

lightened with a knowledge and wifdom revealed to us by God himfelf?

May one not therefore juftly wonder, what it is that could lead any people into an imagination of the abfolute per-fection of *human Reafon?* There feems no more in the ftate of mankind to be-tray a man into this fancy, than to per-fuade him that the reafon of *Infants* is abfolutely perfect. For fenfe and expe-rience are as full and ftrong a proof againft one, as againft the other.

But it muft be faid for thefe writers, that they decline all arguments from facts and experience, to give a better account of human nature ; but with the fame juftice, as if a man were to lay afide the authority of *hiftory*, to give you a truer account of the life of *Alexander*.

They

They argue about the perfection of human Reaſon, not as if it were ſomething *already* in being, that had its nature and *condition*, and ſhewed itſelf to be what it is; but as if it were ſomething that might take its ſtate and condition, according to their fancies and ſpeculations about it.

Their objection againſt Revelation is founded upon the pretended ſufficiency, and abſolute perfection, of the light and ſtrength of human Reaſon, to teach all men all that is wiſe, and holy, and divine, in Religion. But how do they *prove* this perfection of human Reaſon? Do they appeal to Mankind as proofs of this perfection? Do they produce any body of men, in this, or any other age of the world, that without any

aſſiſtance

affiftance from Revelation, have attained
to this perfection of religious knowledge ? This is not fo much as pretended
to : the hiftory of fuch men is entirely
wanting. And yet the want of fuch a
fact as this, has even the force of demon-
ftration againft this pretended fufficiency
of natural Reafon.

Becaufe it is a matter not capable
of any other kind of proof, but muft be
admitted as certainly true, or rejected
as certainly falfe, according as fact and
experience bear witnefs for or againft
it.

For an enquiry about the light, and
ftrength, and fufficiency of Reafon to
guide and preferve men in the knowledge
and practice of true religion, is a queftion, as *folely* to be refolved by *fact and*

Q                              *experience,*

*experience,* as if the enquiry was about the *shape* of man's body, or the *number* of his senses. And to talk of a light and strength of Reason, natural to man, which fact and experience have never yet proved, is as egregious nonsense, as to talk of natural senses, or faculties of his body, which fact and experience have never yet discovered.

For, as the *existence* of man cannot be proved, but from fact and experience ; so every *quality* of man, whether of body or mind, and every degree of that quality, can only be proved by fact and experience.

The degrees of human *strength,* the nature of human *passions ;* the duration of human *life,* the light and strength of human *Reason* in matters of religion, are things not possible to be known in any

*other*

*other degree*, than *so far* as fact and experience prove them.

From the bare confideration of a rational foul in union with a body, and bodily paffions, we can neither prove man to be *strong* or *weak*, *good* or *bad*, *sickly* or *found*, *mortal* or *immortal*: all thefe qualities muft difcover themfelves, as the *eye* difcovers its degree of *fight*, the *hand* its degree of *strength*, &c.

To enquire therefore, whether men have, by nature, light and ftrength fufficient to guide, and keep them in the true religion? is the fame appeal to fact and experience, as to require, whether men are *mortal*, *sickly*, or *found*; or how far they can *see* and *hear*. For nothing that relates to human nature, as a quality of it, can poffibly have any other proof.

If

If some other enquirers into human nature, should affirm, that there is in mankind a *natural inſtinct* of mutual love *ſufficient* to make every man, at all times, love every other man, with the *ſame degree* of affection as he loves himſelf; I ſuppoſe ſuch an opinion would be thought too abſurd and extravagant, to need any confutation. And yet all the abſurdity of it would lie in this, that it affirmed ſomething of the *ſufficiency* of a natural quality in man, which could not be ſupported by a ſingle inſtance of any one man, and was contrary to the experience and hiſtory of every age of the world.

By what has been here ſaid, I hope the reader will obſerve, that this enquiry about the perfection or imperfection, the ſtrength or weakneſs of Reaſon in man, as to matters of religion, reſts

*wholly*

*wholly* upon fact and experience ; and
that therefore all fpeculative reafonings
upon it are to be looked upon as idle and
vifionary, as a fick man's dreams about
health ; and as wholly to be rejected, as
any fpeculative arguments that fhould
pretend to prove, in fpite of all facts and
experience, the *immortality*, and *unalter-*
*able* ftate of human bodies.

---

## CHAP. V.

*Shewing, that all the* mutability *of our tempers, the* diforders *of our paffions, the* corruption *of our hearts, all the* reveries *of the imagination, all the* contradictions *and* abfurdities *that are to be found in human opinions, are ftrictly, and precife-ly the mutability, diforders, corruption, and abfurdities of* human Reafon.

IT is the intent of this chapter to fhew, that although common language af-cribes a variety of faculties and principles to the foul, imputing this action to the blindnefs of our *paffions*, that to the in-conftancy of our *tempers;* one thing to the

heat

heat of our *imagination*, another to the coolnefs of our *reafon ;* yet, in ftrictnefs of truth, every thing that is done by us is the action and operation of our Reafon, and is to be afcribed to it, as the fole faculty or principle from whence it proceeded, and by which it is governed and effected.

Nobody denies, that there is a *Law* or *Light* of Reafon common to men. All this is as freely granted, as that *love* and *hatred, feeling* and *fenfation* are common to men; and is granting no more, than that men are by nature intelligent and rational Beings. For the faculties of man, as he is an intelligent being, as neceffarily perceive fome difference in actions, as to *good* and *bad,* as they perceive fome things they like, and fome things they diflike. In this fenfe, there

is

is a law, or light of Reaſon, common to all men; and the law of Reaſon is in men, as the law of *thinking*, of *liking*, and *diſliking* is in men.

And the different degrees of Reaſon are in men, as the different degrees of love and averſion; as the different degrees of wit, parts, good nature, or ill nature, are in man.

And as all men have naturally more or leſs of theſe qualities, ſo all men have naturally more or leſs of Reaſon: and the bulk of mankind are as different in Reaſon, as they are in theſe qualities.

As Love is the ſame paſſion in all men, yet is infinitely different; as Hatred is the ſame paſſion in all men, yet with infinite differences; ſo Reaſon is the
fame

fame faculty in all men, yet with infinite differences.

And as our Paffions not only make us different from other men, but frequently, and almoft daily, different from our-felves, loving and hating under great inconftancy ; fo our Reafon is not only different from the Reafon of other men, but is often different from itfelf by a ftrange inconftancy, fetting up firft one opinion, and then another.

So that when we talk of *human Rea-fon*, or a Reafon *common* to mankind, we talk of as *various, uncertain*, and *unmea-furable* a thing, as when we talk of a *love*, a *liking*, an *averfion*, a *good nature* or *ill nature*, common to mankind ; for thefe qualities admit of no variation, uncertainty, or mutability, but fuch as they

they directly receive from the *Reason* of mankind.

For it is as much the Reason of man that acts in all thefe tempers, and makes them to be juft what they are, as it is the Reafon of man that demonftrates a mathematical propofition.

Was our Reafon fteady, and of one kind, there would be juft the fame fteadinefs and regularity in our tempers; did not Reafon fall into miftakes, follies and abfurdities, we fhould have nothing foolifh or abfurd in our love or averfion. For every humour, every kind of love or averfion, is as ftrictly the *action* or *operation* of our Reafon, as judgment is the act of our Reafon.

And the tempers and paffions of a child differ only from the tempers and

paffions

paffions of a man, exactly in the fame
degree, as the Reafon of a child differs
from the Reafon of man.

So that our paffions and tempers are
the natural actions and real effects of our
Reafon, and have no qualities, either
good or bad, but fuch as are to be imputed to it.

A laudable good nature, or a laudable
averfion, is only Reafon acting in a *certain manner;* a criminal good nature, or
a criminal averfion, is nothing elfe, but
an ill-judging Reafon; that is, Reafon
acting in another certain manner.

But ftill it is Reafon, or our underftanding, that is the *only agent* in our bad
paffions, as well as good paffions; and
as much the *fole agent* in all our paffions
and tempers, as in things of mere fpeculation.

So that the ſtate of Reaſon in human life, is nothing elſe but the ſtate of human tempers and paſſions; and *right Reaſon* in morality, is nothing elſe but *right love* and *right averſion.*

And all our tempers and ways of liking and diſliking, are as much the acts and operations of our Reaſon, as the wiſeſt actions of our life; and they only differ from Reaſon, as Reaſon differs from itſelf, when it judges rightly, and when it judges erroneouſly.

All that therefore, which we commonly call the weakneſs, blindneſs, and diſorder of our *paſſions,* is in reality the weakneſs, blindneſs, and diſorder of our *Reaſon.* For a right love, or wrong love, denotes only our Reaſon acting in a *certain particular manner.*

So

So that if any thing can be said pre-cisely, or with exactness, of love, aver-sion, good nature or ill nature, as com-mon to mankind ; the same may be said of Reason, as common to mankind.

And, if it would be very foolish and absurd, to ascribe an absolute perfection to human love, making it alone a suffi-cient guide to all good; or an absolute perfection to human hatred, as a suffi-cient preservative from all vice ; it is equally absurd to ascribe the same per-fection to human Reason: because nei-ther love nor hatred have any thing per-fect or imperfect, good or bad in them, but what is solely the action and opera-tion of Reason.

For the distinction of our Reason from our Passions, is only a distinction in

R                    lan-

language, made at pleafure; and is no
more real in the things themfelves, than
the *defire* and *inclination* are really different from the *Will*. All therefore that
is weak and foolifh in our paffions, is the
weaknefs and folly of our Reafon; all
the inconftancy and caprice of our hu-
mours and tempers, is the caprice and
inconftancy of our Reafon.

It is not *Flattery*, that compliments
vice in authority; it is not *Corruption*,
that makes men proftitute their honour;
it is not *Senfuality*, that plunges men into
*Debauchery*; it is not *Avarice*, that makes
men fordid; it is not *Ambition*, that
makes them reftlefs; it is not *Bribery*,
that makes men fell their confciences;
it is not *Intereſt*, that makes them lie and
cheat, and perjure themfelves. What

is

is it therefore? Why, it is *Reason*, the *use of Reason, human Reason*, that does all this.

To suppose that Reason permits itself to be governed by passions or tempers, but is not the *immediate, full agent* of all that is done by them, is as absurd, as to suppose that Reason permits itself to be governed by the *hand* when it is writing falsely, or the *tongue* when it is talking profanely, but is not the immediate, direct agent of all that is written and spoken by them.

*Brutes* are incapable of imprudence and immorality, because none of their actions are the actions of *Reason*: every thing therefore that is imprudence, immorality, baseness, or villany in us, must be the act of our Reason; otherwise it

could

could no more be imprudent or immoral, than the actions of brutes.

If, therefore, Reason be the only faculty that diftinguifheth us from brutes; it neceffarily follows, that thofe irregularities, whether of humour, paffions, or tempers, which cannot be imputed to brutes, muft be folely attributed to that faculty by which we are diftinguifhed from brutes; and confequently, every thing that is foolifh, vain, fhameful, falfe, treacherous, and bafe, muft be the fole exprefs acts of our Reafon; fince, if they were the acts of any thing elfe, they could have no more vanity, falfhood, or bafenefs, than hunger and thirft.

As therefore all that is faithful, juft, and wife, can only be attributed to that

which.

which is done by our Reafon; fo, by plain confequence, all that is vain, falfe, or fhameful, can only be imputed to any acts, as they are the acts of Reafon.

. It is not my intent in the leaft to cenfure or condemn our common language, which confiders and talks of Reafon and the Paffions, as if. they were as different as a *governor* and his *fubjects*.

Thefe forms of fpeech are very intelligible and ufeful, and give great life and ornament to all difcourfes upon morality; and are even neceffary both for the Hiftorian, the Poet, and the Orator.

But, when certain perfons afcribe to human Reafon, as a *diftinct faculty* of. human nature, I know not what *perfection*, it is neceffary to confider human. Reafon and human Nature, not as it is

repre-

reprefented in common language, but as
it is in reality in itfelf.

Notwithftanding, therefore, in common language, our Paffions, and the
effects of them, are very ufefully diftinguifhed from our Reafon, I have here
ventured to fhew, that all the diforders
of human nature, are precifely the diforders of human Reafon ; and that all the
perfection or imperfection of our paffions, is nothing elfe but the perfection
or imperfection of our Reafon.

And we may as well think, that judgment, prudence, difcretion, are things
different from our Reafon, as that humour, temper, approbation, or averfion,
are really different from our Reafon.

For, as it is a right exercife of Reafon, that denominates its actions to be
*Prudence, Judgment,* and *Difcretion;* fo it
is

is a wrong exercife of Reafon, that denominates its actions to be *Humour, Temper,*
and *Caprice.*

And it would be as abfurd to condemn humour and caprice, if they were
not the actions and operations of Reafon,
as to commend a prudence and difcretion, that were the effects of an irrational
principle.

Our follies, therefore, and abfurdities
of every kind, are as neceffarily to be
afcribed to our Reafon, as the *firft, immediate,* and *fole* Caufe of them, as our
wifdom and difcretion are to be afcribed
to it in that degree.

The difference betwixt Reafon affent-
ing to the properties of a *fquare,* and
Reafon acting in motions of *defire* or
*averfion,* is only this, that in the latter
cafe it is Reafon, acting under a fenfe of
good

*good* or *evil*, in the former cafe, it is
Reafon acting under a fenfe of *magnitude*.

And as the relations of magnitude, as
they are the objects of our Reafon, are
only the objects of its *affent* or *diffent;* fo
good and evil, as they are objects of our
Reafon, are only the objects of its *defire* or *averfion:* and as the affent or diffent, in matters of fpeculation, whether right or wrong, is folely the act of
our Reafon; fo defire or averfion, in
human life, whether right or wrong, is
equally the act of our Reafon.

All the good, therefore, that there is
in any of our defires or averfions, is the
good of our Reafon; and all the evil or
blindnefs there is in any of our paffions,
is folely the evil and blindnefs of our
Reafon.

Becaufe

Becaufe love, defire, averfion, denote nothing elfe but our Reafon acting in a certain manner; juft as prudence, difcretion, and judgment, denote nothing elfe but our Reafon acting in a certain manner.

We often fay, that our Paffions deceive us, or perfuade us; but this is no more ftrictly fo, than when we fay, our *intereft* deceived, or a *bribe* blinded us. For bribes and intereft are not active principles, nor have any power of deception; it is only our Reafon that gives them a falfe value, and prefers them to a greater good.

It is juft fo, in what we call the deceit of our Paffions: they meddle with us no more than bribes meddle with us; but that pleafurable perception, which is to be found in certain enjoyments, is by

our

our Reafon preferred to that better good, which we might expect from a felf-denial.

We fay again, that our Paffions paint things in falfe colours, and prefent to our minds vain appearances of happinefs.

But this is no more ftrictly true, than when we fay, our *Imagination* forms caftles in the air. For the imagination fignifies no diftinct faculty from our Reafon, but only, Reafon acting upon our *own ideas.*

So, when our Paffions are faid to give falfe colours to things, or prefent vain appearances of happinefs, it is only our Reafon acting upon its own ideas of *good* and *evil*, juft as it acts upon its own ideas of *architecture*, in forming caftles in the air.

So that, all that which we call different faculties of the foul, tempers and paffions

of

of the heart, ftrictly fpeaking, means nothing elfe but the various acts and operations of one and the fame rational
principle; which has different names,
according to *the objects* which it acts
upon, and *the manner* of its acting.

In fome things it is called fpeculative,
in others it is called practical Reafon.
And we may as juftly think our fpeculative Reafon is a different faculty from
our practical Reafon, as that our tempers,
averfions, or likings, are not as fully and
folely to be afcribed to our Reafon, as
fyllogifms and demonftrations.

For, it is our Reafon alone that chufes
the true good; fo it is our Reafon alone
that chufes the falfe good: as it is Reafon alone that is the agent, when purity
and integrity are preferred to fenfual
pleafure, and fecular advantage; fo it is

4

our Reafon alone that is the agent, when
fenfual pleafure, and fecular advantage,
are preferred to purity and integrity.

For the fame Principle, which is the
agent of all that is good in us, muft be
equally the agent of all that is evil.

All virtue is nothing elfe, but Reafon
acting in a certain manner; and all vice
is nothing elfe, but Reafon acting in a
certain contrary manner. All the difference is in the actions, and none at all
in the agent.

And to fay, that Reafon acts in our
virtues, and Paffion acts in our vices,
is as abfurd, as to fay the contrary, that
Paffion is the agent in our virtues, and
Reafon the agent in our vices. For the
action or power of Reafon is as much
required to make any thing vicious, as
to make any thing virtuous.

Every

Every thing therefore that is chofen, whether it be good or bad, is the exprefs act and operation of Reafon.

Reafon therefore is certainly the worft, as well as the beft faculty that we have: as it is the only principle of virtue, fo it is, as certainly, the fole caufe of all that is bafe, horrid, and fhameful in human life. As it alone can difcover truth, fo it alone leads us into the groffeft errors.

It was as truly Reafon that made *Medea* kill her children, that made *Cato* kill himfelf, that made pagans offer human facrifices to idols; that made *Epicurus* deny a providence, *Mahomet* pretend a revelation; that made fome men fcepticks, others bigots; fome enthufiafts, others profane; that made *Hobbes* affert all religion to be human invention, and *Spinofa* to declare trees, and ftones, and

S                animals,

animals, to be parts of God; that makes
Free-thinkers deny freedom of will, and
Fatalifts exhort to a reformation of manners; that made *Vaux* a confpirator, and
*Ludlow* a regicide; that made *Muggle-
ton* a fanatic, and *Rochefter* a libertine:
it was as truly human Reafon that did
all thefe things, as it is human Reafon
that demonftrates mathematical propofi-
tions.

For as all miftakes in fpeculation are
as much the acts and operation of Reafon, as true conclufions; fo all errors in
duty, whether civil or religious, are as
much the acts of our Reafon, as the exercife of the moft folid virtues.

*Medea* and *Cato* acted as truly according to the judgment of their Reafon,
at that time, as the *Confeffor* that
chufes

2

chufes rather to fuffer, than deny his
faith.

And the difference betwixt them does
not confift in this, that one power or faculty of the mind, acted in one of them,
and another faculty, or power of the
mind, acted in another; that is, that
Reafon acted in one, and Paffion in another; but purely in the different *ftate* of
their Reafon. For had not *Medea* and
*Cato* thought it beft to do what they did,
at the time they did it, they would no
more have done it, than the *Confeffor*
would chufe to fuffer rather than deny
his faith, unlefs he had judged it beft fo
to do.

It may indeed be well enough faid in
common language, that Paffion made
*Medea* and *Cato* to do as they did, juft as
it may be faid of a man that affirms a

*plenum,*

*plenum,* or holds any fpeculative abfurdity, that it is blindnefs or prejudice that keeps him in it. Not as if blindnefs or prejudice were powers or faculties of his mind, but as they fignify the *ill ftate* of his Reafon. Juft fo the paffions may be faid to govern men in their actions; not as if they were powers of the mind, but as they denote the difordered ftate of Reafon. And whenever any thing is imputed to the ftrength and violence of our Paffions, ftrictly fpeaking, it only means the weaknefs and low condition of our Reafon at that time.

For Reafon governs as fully when our actions and tempers are ever fo bad, as it does when our actions and tempers are found and good. And the only difference

rence is, that Reason acting well, governs in the one case, and Reason acting ill, governs in the other.

Just as it is the same Reason, that
• sometimes judges strictly right, which at other times judges exceeding wrong, in matters of speculation.

When therefore we say, that Reason governs the passions, it means no more, in strict truth, than that Reason governs itself; that it acts with deliberation and attention; does not yield to its first judgments or opinions, but uses second, and third thoughts.

So that, guarding against the Passions, is only guarding against its own first judgments and opinions; that is, guarding against itself.

To all this it may, perhaps, be objected, that our passions and tempers arise
from

from bodily motions, and depend very much upon the ſtate of our blood and animal ſpirits; and that, therefore, what we do under their commotions, cannot be attributed to our Reaſon.

It is readily granted, that the body has this ſhare in our paſſions and tempers: but then the ſame thing muſt be granted of the body, in all the acts and operations of the mind. So that if our deſires and averſions cannot be imputed to our Reaſon, as its acts, becauſe of the joint operation of the animal ſpirits in them; no more can ſyllogiſms and demonſtrations be attributed to our Reaſon as its operations, becauſe the operation of bodily ſpirits concurreth in the forming of them.

For the moſt abſtract thought, and calm ſpeculation of the mind, has as truly

truly the *concurrence*, and *conjunct* operation of bodily fpirits, as our ftrongeft
defires or averfions. And it is as much
owing to the ftate of the body that fuch
. fpeculations are what they are, as it is
owing to the ftate of the body that fuch
paffions are what they are.

For the motions of the bodily fpirits
are infeparable from, and according to,
the ftate and action of the mind : when
Reafon is in fpeculation of a trifle, they
concur but *weakly ;* when Reafon fpecu-
lates intenfely, their operation is *increafed.* And fometimes the attention
of the mind is fo great, and has fo engaged and called in all the animal fpirits to its affiftance, that the operations
of our fenfes are fufpended, and we
neither fee nor feel, till the attention of
the

the mind has let the fpirits return to all parts of the body.

Now, will any one fay, that thefe intenfe thoughts are lefs the acts of the mind, becaufe they have a greater concurrence of bodily fpirits than when it is acting with indifference, and fo has a leffer quantity of bodily fpirits?

Yet this might as well be faid, as to fay, that the affent or diffent, in fpeculation, is the act of our Reafon; but liking or difliking, loving or hating, are not fo the acts of our Reafon, becaufe they have a greater concurrence, and different motions of bodily fpirits.

For, as the mind is in a different ftate when it defires good, or fears evil, from what it is when it only compares two triangles; fo the motions or concurrence of the bodily fpirits have only *fuch* a dif-

ference

ference as is ftrictly *correfpondent* to thefe two ftates of the mind. They act and join as much in comparing the triangles, as in the defire of good, or fear of evil. And the mind is juft fo much governed by the body, in its paffions, as it is governed by it in its calmeft contemplations.

For as the gentle quiet operation of the animal fpirits is then ftrictly correfpondent, and entirely owing to the ftate and action of the mind ; fo in all our paffions, the ftrong and increafed motion of the animal fpirits is then ftrictly correfpondent, and entirely owing to the ftate and action of the mind.

So that Reafon is neither more nor lefs the agent in all our tempers and paffions, than it is in our moft dry and fedate fpeculations.

It

It may, and often does happen, that a man may have as great an eagernefs and impatience in the folving a mathematical problem, as another hath to obtain any great good, or avoid any great evil.

But may it therefore be faid, that it is not Reafon that folves, or defires to folve, the problem, becaufe the bodily fpirits are fo active in it?

In a word; if our paffions and tempers might not be imputed to our Reafon, as its own genuine acts and operations, be-caufe they have fuch a concurrence of bodily fpirits, neither could arguing, or reafoning, be attributed to our *Reafon*, as its proper act and operation, becaufe in all argumentation the bodily fpirits are neceffarily employed; and the better and clofer the reafoning is, the more they are excited and employed.

If

If it fhould farther be objected, that Reafon is only *right Reafon*, and therefore cannot be faid to act or operate, but where, and fo far, as right Reafon acts.

This is as abfurd as to fay, that *Love* fignifies only *pure love*, and *Hatred* juft hatred ; and that therefore a man cannot be faid to love or hate, but when, and fo far, as his love is pure, and his hatred juft.—

To draw now fome plain confequen-ces from the foregoing account.

*Firft*, If Reafon be, as above repre-fented, the *univerfal Agent ;* if all the difference amongft men, either in fpecu-lation or practice, be only fuch a diffe-rence as Reafon makes, then nothing can be more extravagant, than to affirm any thing concerning the degree of per-fection

fection or imperfection of Reafon, as common to man. It is as wild and romantic, as to pretend to ftate the meafure of Folly and Wifdom, of Fear and Courage, of Pride and Humility, of good Humour and ill Humour, common to Mankind : for as thefe ftates of the Mind are only fo many different ftates of Reafon, fo no uncertainty belongs to them, but what, in the *fame degree*, belongs to *Reafon*.

*Secondly*, Granting that all matters of Religion muft be agreeable to *right*, *unprejudiced* Reafon; yet this could be no ground for receiving nothing in religion, but what *human* Reafon could prove to be neceffary : for *human* Reafon is no more *right unprejudiced* Reafon,

Reafon, than a finner is *finlefs*, or a man an *angel*.

Granting again, that a man may go a great way towards rectifying his Reafon, and laying afide its prejudices; yet no particular man can be a *better judge* of the rectitude of his *own Reafon*, than he is of the rectitude of his own *felf-love*, the fagacity of his own *underftanding*, the brightnefs of his own *parts*, the juftnefs of his own *eloquence*, and the depth of his own *judgment*.

For there is nothing to deceive him in *felf-love*, in the opinion of his *own merit*, *wit*, *judgment* and *eloquence*, but what has the fame power to deceive him, in the opinion of his own Reafon. And, if *it be the fate of moft fects to be fondeft of their uglieft brats*, none feem fo inevitably expofed to this *fatality*, as thofe, whofe Religion is to

T                                have

have no *form*, but such as it receives from their own hearts.

*Thirdly,* A man that has his Religion to chuse, and with this previous privilege, that he need not allow any thing to be matter of religion, but what his own Reason can prove to be so, is in as fair a way to be governed by his *Passions,* as he that has his *condition* of life to chuse, with the liberty of taking that, which his own Reason directs him to.

Does any one suppose now, that nothing but *right Reason* would direct him in the choice of his condition? Or that he would make the better choice, because he proceeded upon this maxim, that nothing could be right, but that which was agreeable to his *own Reason?* Or that his temper, his prejudices, his self-love, his

passions,

paffions, his partiality, would have no influence upon his choice, becaufe he had refigned himfelf up to his *own Reafon.*

For as our choice of a condition of life is not a matter of fpeculation, but of good and evil; fo however it is recommended to our Reafon, it chiefly excites our paffions; and our choice will be juft as reafonable, as our tempers and paffions are. And he, who is made the moft pofitive of the fufficiency of his own Reafon, will be the moft likely to be governed by the blindnefs of his own Paffions.

Now it is juft the fame in the choice of a Religion, as in the choice of a condition of life: as it is not a matter of fpeculation, but of *good* and *evil*; fo, if

it

it be left to be stated and determined by our *own Reason*, it rather appeals to our Tempers, than employs our Reason; and to resign ourselves up to our own Reason, to tell us what ought or not to be a matter of Religion, is only re-signing ourselves up to our Tempers to take what we *like*, and refuse what we *dislike* in Religion.

For, it is not only natural and easy for him, who believes that nothing can be a part of Religion, but what his Reason can prove necessary to be so, to take that to be *fully proved*, which is only *mightily liked*; and all that to be entire-ly contrary to *Reason*, which is only vastly contrary to his *Tempers*; this, I say, is not only natural and easy to hap-pen, but scarce possible to be avoided.

In

In a word; when *Self-love* is a proper arbitrator betwixt a man and his adverſary; when *Revenge* is a juſt judge of Meekneſs; when *Pride* is a true lover of Humility; when *Falſhood* is a teacher of Truth; when *Luſt* is a faſt friend of Chaſtity; when the *Fleſh* leads to the Spirit; when *Senſuality* delights in Self-denial; when *Partiality* is a promoter of Equity; when the *Palate* can taſte the difference between Sin and Holineſs; when the *Hand* can feel the truth of a Propoſition, then may *human Reaſon* be a proper Arbitrator between God and Man; the ſole, final, juſt Judge of all that ought, or ought not to be matter of a *Holy*, *Divine*, and *Heavenly* Religion.——

Again: if this be the ſtate of Reaſon, as has been fully proved; if all we be- lieve

lieve or difbelieve, love or hate, chufe
or refufe; if all that is wife or abfurd,
holy or profane, glorious or fhameful,
in thought, word, or deed, be to be imputed to it; then, it is as grofs an abfurdity to talk of the perfection of *human
Reafon*, as, of the unfpotted holinefs of
*human Life*, the abfolute purity of *human Love*, the immutable juftice of *human Hatred*, and the infallibility of *human
Conjectures*.

*Laftly*, To pretend that our Reafon is
too perfect to be governed by any thing
but its own light, is the fame extravagance, as to pretend, that our love is
*too pure* to be governed by any thing but
its own inclinations, our hatred *too juft*
to be governed by any thing but its
own motions.   For, if all that is bafe
and criminal in love, all that is unjuft
and

and wicked in hatred, be ſtrictly and
ſolely to be imputed to our Reaſon ;
then, no perfection can be aſcribed to
our Reaſon, but ſuch as is to be aſcribed
. to our love and hatred.


F I N I S.

The following Books may be had of

# R. EDWARDS, BOOKSELLER,

## No. 142, *BOND-STREET.*

COMPLETE SETS OF THE

VOYAGE Pittorefque de Naples & Sicile 5 vols large Folio.

Voyage Pittorefque de la Suiffe, 5 vols large Folio.

Voyage Pittorefque de la France, 4 vols large Folio.

Tableau de l'Empire Othoman, par Monf. de M . . . . D'Ohffon, avec des Planches fuperbes, 2 vols, large Folio.

Sir William Hamilton's Account of the Volcanos of the Two Sicilies, with 63 Prints, coloured from the original Drawings, 3 vols.

Piranefi's Roman Antiquities and Ruins, 4 vols in 136 Plates, finely engraved.

Adams's Ruins of Spalatro in Dalmatia, with 61 Engravings, chiefly by Bartolozzi.

Sir William Hamilton's Etrufcan, Greek and Roman Antiquities, on the ancient Vafes found at Herculaneum and Pompeii, now in the Britifh Mufeum, coloured from the Originals.

Walton's

# B O O K S, &c.

Walton's Edition of the Polyglott Bible, with Castell's Lexicon, 8 vols.

Vitringa's Commentary on Isaiah, 2 vols.

Poli Synopsis Criticorum, 5 vols.

Physique Sacrée, being a Natural History of the Bible, by Sheutzer, with 750 Prints by Pfeffel, very fine Impressions, 8 vols.

Mortier's Cuts to the Bible, 2 vols very fine Impressions.

Aldrovandi Opera Omnia, 13 vols. the *best Edition*.

Houbraken's Heads of Illustrious Persons, with their Lives by Birch, *the first Impressions*, on large Paper, splendidly bound in Morocco.

The Illustrious Persons of France, with their Portraits and Lives, by Perrault, 2 vols.

The best Editions of Calvin, Luther, Erasmus, &c.

Henry on the Bible, 5 vols, the best Edition.

Grævius & Gronovius's Greek, Roman, and Sicilian Antiquities.

Catalogo de gli Antichi Monumenti di Ercolano.

Horsley's Britannia Romana.

Antiquities of Pozzuoli, Palmyra, &c.

Voyages to the South Sea, &c. by Hawkesworth, Cook, Forster, Wilson, Dixon, and Portlock, in 14 vols, elegantly bound in Russia; with 2 Atlas Folio Volumes of Plates, and Duplicate Proof Impressions to most of the Prints in Cook's last Voyage—*a matchless Set.*

Tableux

# B O O K S, &c.

Tableaux Topographiques Pittorefques & Hiſto-
riques de la Suiſſe, in 12 vols, elegantly bound
in Morocco.

Buffon (Comte de) toutes ſes Ouvres d'Hiſtoire Na-
turelle, 35 vols, *the Beſt Edition.*

Edwards's Natural Hiſtory of Birds, the original
Edition, coloured by the Author, 7 vols,
elegant, in Morocco

Wilke's Hiſtory of Moths and Butterflies, with the
Plants on which they feed, beautifully co-
loured; the original Edition, elegant, in
Morocco.

Albin's Natural Hiſtory of Engliſh Inſects, beſt
Edition, coloured by the Author, with the
Addition of Derham's Notes on *Albin*,
elegant.

Pennant's Britiſh Zoology, 4 vols, with 284 Plates
of Quadrupeds, Birds, Fiſhes, and Shells,
beautifully coloured, and elegantly bound in
Morocco.

A complete Set of the Philoſophical Tranſactions at
large, 74 vols, bound in Morocco

Worlidge's Select Collection of Drawings, from
Antique Gems, in 183 Plates, with his Por-
trait; the Meduſa, &c. large Paper, elegantly bound in 2 Volumes, Morocco.

Wood's Eſſay on the Genius and Writings of Homer,
boards, uncut.

Lavater, Eſſai ſur la Phyſiognomie, 3 vols. (*the beſt
Edition*) elegantly bound in Morocco.

Bryant's

# B O O K S, &c.

Bryant's Ancient Mythology, 3 vol. elegantly bound.

Hawkefworth's Telemachus.

The Medallic Hiſtory of England, from the Conqueſt to the Revolution, on 40 Copperplates.

Lady Rachel Ruſſell's Letters, handſomely bound.

Views of Gentlemen's Seats in England and Wales.

The Claſſics which have been printed at the Parma Preſs.

Edwards's Edition of the Caſtle of Otranto, beautifully printed by Bodoni, at Parma.

———————————————

☞ French Books of Reputation regularly imported.—Foreign Books of Prints, and Antiquities, and Books of Hiſtory, Science, &c. in all Languages, may be had as above, of the beſt Editions, and in the moſt elegant Variety of Bindings.